BELMONT
Story Review

EDITOR
Richard Sowienski

POETRY EDITOR
Gary McDowell

FOUNDING EDITORS
Sam Denlinger, Krista Walsh, Ethan Blackbird, Jennifer Cantrell,
Caroline George, Katherine Puckett

SENIOR ADVISORS
Jennifer Cantrell
Sam Denlinger
Krista Walsh

ADVISORS
Leah Bruce, Allison Gerber, Hannah Marie Lamb, Kathryn Notestine,
Lindsay Hunnicutt, Rhondje Singh Tanwar, Matt Hollingsworth,
Melissa Deanna Kriz, Alivia Baker, Claire Harmeyer, Samantha Rodriguez,
Katherine Foreman, Savannah Morrow

DESIGNERS
Leah Bruce and Allison Gerber
Nameplate design: Journey Global Media

Belmont Story Review is produced through Belmont University's Publishing Program.

CONTACT
Richard Sowienski, Publishing Program Director
1900 Belmont Blvd.
Nashville, TN 37212
E-mail: belmontstoryreview@gmail.com

TABLE *of* CONTENTS

Susan M. Gelles

Samuel Martin

TABLE *of* CONTENTS

F. Daniel Rzicznek

A. J. Odasso

Keith Montesano

Exploring Liminal States

Welcome to the premiere issue of *Belmont Story Review*. It's been quite a journey from the concept to our first call for submissions to our first accepted piece to the completed issue. The issue's theme, Liminal States, reflects that process of becoming, a process of moving from one state to another, a "standing on the threshold."

Our first accepted submission, "The Cattle Guard" by Jesse van Eerden, inspired the theme. In the essay, van Eerden reflects on the state of her marriage and a childhood memory of growing up on a farm:

> I write now about the calf caught because the image of liminality feels so accurate to grief. From the Latin, *limina* means threshold, the in-between place outside of the familiar but not yet inside a new possibility. The liminal place is the coarse rusted place, the desert, the scrub, the place that catches your little hooves in the cattle guard ruts and you are unable to go forward though you are pulled, and unable to return though you want more than anything else to do so.

The issue theme, however, did not emerge until all the stories and poetry had been gathered and we looked for a connecting thread. The idea of "liminal states," perhaps not surprising given the rapidity of technological change, the shifting of cultural norms, the upheaval in the political process, found expression throughout the soon-to-be-published submissions of prose and poetry.

Stories of liminality

In "The Cadillac Man," Eric Lloyd Blix begins his story by telling of the transition of ownership of a piece of Indian land that once "belonged only to the wildlife and the sacred maker," and had become over time a pioneer outpost, a dumping ground, a vacant lot and now a scrap heap. The story, one may argue, explores the liminality between sacred and profane, and it explores the power of naming.

Susan Gelles, in "The Noon Executions," brings us the character of Antonio, the state-appointed calligrapher (in a setting reminiscent of a García Márquez story). He finds himself on the threshold between that of interrogator and interrogated, listener and storyteller.

Jumping to the very real and often painful present, English professor Sam Martin finds himself in that liminal state of being "right-sized": fired but still employed. Martin's essay, "The Death of Baldr," in a Montaigne-like exploration, considers parenthood and loss through Norse myth, specifically Odin foreseeing the death of his son Baldr. The story of Odin and Baldr appears in *The Voluspo*, which was arguably written by a tenth-century "pagan Icelander with knowledge of Christianity," writes Martin. "In other words: a writer living in a clash of tales—an age between ages, like our own..."—more liminality.

Our other stories convey states of chaos, flux, transition. An elderly man on his deathbed tells his wife that his profession of Christianity was made only to gain her hand in marriage ("Veldon," Scott Kaukonen); a Japanese-American woman engaged to a Korean-American questions her love and their future as missionaries ("Unspeakable Joy," E.K. Ota); two young brothers seek escape into an imaginary world as a buttress to their divorced mother's sadness ("Birds in the Head," Tonia Payne); an essayist contemplates the heaviness and silence of death ("Listen to the Silence," Lisa Laughlin). Translator Patricia Worth brings us a tale of forgiveness and otherness—a queen births a princess-frog ("The Mandrake," Jean Lorrain's 1899 story).

Our poetry features authors F. Daniel Rzicznek, Mark Baumer, A.J. Odasso, and Keith Montesano. In his poem "Into the Void," Montesano speaks directly to our theme: "And at night the crescendo/of a million turned-on faucets, where liminal becomes nothing/but the darkness of places/even the mind can't touch."

About the magazine

At the very beginning of this process, I wondered if the world needed another literary magazine. There are many fine magazines already out there, including *The Missouri Review*, where I had the pleasure of serving as managing editor for five years. Since then, the world of publishing has become increasingly complex. Could the Belmont Publishing Program, with its initial handful of majors, pull this off? On further reflection, I thought there was no better way to learn about the publishing industry—truly in a liminal state—than to thrust students into the operation of all facets of journal operations: editorial, author relations, public relations, marketing, scheduling, design, social media, and the managing of dozens of other details needed to get the issue published.

And furthermore, how could one go wrong by providing another venue for literary talent, those with established reputations and those beginning their careers. But if we were to publish, I did insist on a few rules. First, authors would be paid, even if only a small amount to begin with. Second, we would be both a digital and print magazine. And finally, though our core will be short stories, creative nonfiction, and poetry, we will pursue creative reportage in areas affiliated with Nashville and Belmont programs, including the subject areas of publishing (read Krista Walsh's interview on ghostwriters), music, film, creativity and collaboration, entertainment, and the intersection of faith and culture.

Of course, matters of faith and culture will be integral to the magazine since we are part of a Christian community. That doesn't mean we publish "Christian literature." We publish writers encountering difficult ideas, writers who see humanity in the context of a fallen world, a world filled with struggles and pain, but also a world of redemption and grace, of the mystical and sacred. Yes, there may be stories where characters act or speak in ways inappropriate for our classrooms, but they are true to the portrayals of situations and characters. My hope is that, when taken as a whole, our stories point to the greater Truth.

Please enjoy the premiere issue of *Belmont Story Review*.

Richard Sowienski
Editor

The CATTLE GUARD

Jessie van Eerden

It happens on the stretch of road where everything happens, all of the significant events that fill childhood time to the brim. On this same stretch I ride the blue bike, fixed on my sister's back as she speeds before me on her yellow banana-seat cruiser past our neighbor's place—Mary Jane's—past the cattle guard at the mouth of her gravel drive, both of us aware that Mary Jane has the Spirit deeply and soundly lodged within her, and today we have learned she has a brain tumor lodged the same. It's this road we cross with ice cream buckets to steal into the labyrinth of wild blackberry bushes where we get a whiff of a copperhead and bolt. It's here where my brother wrecks his racer into barbed wire and his long cut pusses up on his back with peroxide, and some thought of death breaks into my tiny invincible head with dread as absolute as his brave, pained whimper. And my other brother crosses this same eminent stretch of road to the field, with a mail-ordered Sears telescope that catches the moon for only a moment, since the moon, when brought down into our manageable universe and sucked into the telescope tube against the naked eye, becomes a fast mover. Even the event of God takes place on this road down which I walk the mile to church in late summer, in jelly shoes cutting blisters, thumbing out one milkweed hull prematurely so the milk-wet silks stick to my arms, and another one more discerningly: it's dry to downiness, and my thumb threads through to set loose the fluff-seeds to propagate, and I get the notion that God is as intimate and touchable as the milkweed hull, infecting people like Mary Jane with visions and, I suppose, tumors, and giving way to my forceful thumb all the same. It is on this road that the calf gets caught in the cattle guard.

It is cold and I wear a snap-up rainbow vest, a boy's hat. The calf, a Guernsey heifer, is tied by its halter to the black pickup's hitch to be guided home, and I sit on the tire hump in the truck bed thinking it a perfect seat for me, the way children see everything held out just for them because they belong so deeply to their own lives. All four of us kids are in the truck bed, I the youngest. I feel the thrum-hum of tires slowly crossing the ridges of the cattle guard that is meant to keep cows from lumbering from the pasture into the road, but here we are crossing the trap with a calf pulled along behind us. The calf resists but is pulled forward and must step her tiny hooves into the ruts where she gets stuck and there is still the forward tug of the pickup. The rope goes taut, the truck keeps going, the calf's neck grows longer and I grow confused on the tire hump then distressed at the rigid rope and rigid neck and strained halter holding stubbornly, and the four of us scream to my father in the truck cab to stop—the calf's eyes going larger—surely he has forgotten about the cattle guard, thinking about all the other things that fathers think about when finally given some solitude. All breath sucks in and tension runs from calf flank up the spine to the elongated neck and wet pink velvet nose heaving, all the way to our open hands slapping the back window of the cab until he turns to see what all the racket is about.

That is all I can remember of this scene, where I sit now at my desk.

Except I know the calf's leg does not splinter; alarm does not mature into horror, not on this day. But I don't know what does happen next, nor do I know what happened beforehand.

Maybe we'd bought the calf from Whitehair who owned the field surrounding Mary Jane's house, or maybe this was a calf of ours that had shimmied through the lax barbed wire fence and we were retrieving her. And maybe we were taking her to the barn to love on and bottle feed because weaning hadn't quite been accomplished, or taking her right to the butcher for winter veal, though at that time my mother told me we traded calves for meat and I believed her. Probably it was in fact one of Dolly's calves and as my mother milked Dolly in the evenings I would have pressed my ear to the swollen bovine hide to listen to her pregnancy. And probably we got the calf home after the incident and tied her to the clothesline pole as we played wiffle ball, and we fed her ribey little apples from the tree in the yard. And surely, in time, she went to the butcher.

But how did we get her out of that fix? Perhaps my father mercifully cut the tether, gathered the heifer in his arms, and carried her home. Perhaps my exasperated father did that and the calf acquiesced, went slack against his chest. But I don't know that that happened. The cattle guard scene exists as if held in a clear mushy globe, or sac, intact, with no before or after, and it exists as an image: a calf's breakable furry body pulled forward but she cannot go, resisting but she cannot go back, for the knobby legs are caught in the ruts. Frozen like this in memory, the hot seizure of time and movement offers no way out. There is nowhere to go. It is a moment of impossibility, so it becomes for me—in the harsh bawling-out of the calf—a dramatization, or a tableau, of grieving.

I have both moved forward and moved back, literally. I lived in West Virginia for the first twenty-two years of my life, lived away for twelve years, and abruptly moved back—three years ago now, in the midst of divorce—to within an hour and a half drive of my childhood home. I was once again driving the curvy roads too fast with familiar ease, wondering, around each bend, if I might run into a younger, more whole version of myself. I took a tenure-track job with retirement and moved into a one-bedroom rental house I get flowers for weekly; I took up with a hound from the local shelter who claimed me, and I took some pleasure in being able to afford good cheese and good wine. But my interior state was bankrupt, everything was wrecked by the divorce, irreparable, and privately I dissolved daily into stupefying tears that wrung me dry until the crying was more like dry heaving. I missed my husband, I missed my life.

I remember one night, in the last month of our marriage, as my husband and I made our way east on the highway, unable to recognize our lives anymore or to name love or sadness or regret by their simple names, and I sat on a linoleum floor in a motel bathroom, under buzzing fluorescence, and it was cold, it was January—in Nevada, I think—with my husband becoming not my husband on the other side of the wall, shivering like a bird as if still outside and not in the cheap room, and I said to someone or something, Stop pulling—I cannot move. Everything felt too hot to touch, as if I were surrounded by glowing stove-burner coils and so could not budge, and as if I were engulfed in air that was somehow barbed when I breathed it, but I had no choice but to breathe it. We could not find a way forward in marriage, nor could we return to what we had been. This seized-up feeling is likely familiar to any newly divorced person. There was no way out.

But of course, I do not write this on a motel bathroom floor. Somehow I got here, to this desk, to this three-years-later self. And the movement baffles me.

Recently, when visiting my parents who still live in the house where I grew up, I walked my dog up that significant stretch of road and found mud and gravel filling the obsolete cattle guard ruts at the top of Mary Jane's drive, since the cows, and Mary Jane herself, are now long gone and someone grows corn in the fields there and had just harvested with a huge combine that had left the stalks all chewed and apocalyptic-looking. This spot once vast enough to hold all the volumes of my little life—such a rich storehouse of memory—was now strung with a useless fencerow and shrunken to a blip of rural landscape. I felt the constriction of time as well as its lording-over. Time regards no event or place worth stopping for. I had to get going, I had a lot of work to do for the new demanding job. I had an empty house waiting for me.

I write now about the calf caught because the image of liminality feels so accurate to grief. From the Latin, *limina* means threshold, the in-between place outside of the familiar but not yet inside a new possibility. The liminal place is the coarse rusted place, the desert, the scrub, the place that catches your little hooves in the cattle guard ruts and you are unable to go forward though you are pulled, and unable to return though you want more than anything else to do so. It is the place of exile from your life and is not a place we ever choose to go, though most of us will admit that going there teaches us what nothing else can and brings on a baptism into being human that cannot happen when we remain in control, riding our days with relative ease and success. Liminality is the crucible for a rough rebirth that involves relinquishing the aggregate gain of what you thought was hard-won knowledge and the security of your shored-up self. Until exile, I never questioned whether or not I loved my life because I'd never regarded it from the outside. Now, a permission is required to let myself love it; effort is required to let myself love it.

All spiritual traditions probably push us toward the threshold, the place of not-knowing. In my tradition, there is the biblical Noah whom I can see frozen in that moment, unable to run out the ark's door last-minute, back to the world of the damned he was born to, and also unable, in that moment, to turn toward a God whose floodwater would fill the lungs of every baby field mouse that wasn't one of the two on the ark of salvation—the impossible moment of envisioning the mice-babies paddling for the sky, God looking on, their paws the size of matchstick heads, until the black water would drown them while Noah would be safe, afloat. Or Lot's wife from later in the Book of Genesis, fleeing the cursed city of Sodom—but then frozen, unable to return to the life she knew, but unable to follow her husband up the hill to safety. It's a liminal moment of grieving—for a microsecond or an eternity—before she turns, somehow chooses to turn and look back, knowing the consequences, and her skin crystallizes to salt, maybe her lungs metamorphosing first, or her eyes, her heart. The kernel of these stories burns brightly with the moment of change and loss of everything, the moment that forges the soul in fire. And liminality can stretch to forty years in the desert for the wandering ex-slaves; it can be downright interminable for Job with his sense of self peeling off painfully with each layer of his leprous skin. And it seems to me that, contrary to the sermonizing of these stories, they do not reveal lessons easy to articulate.

*

I also write about the calf because I am not there now, at the threshold, though I cannot say that I am on the other side of it either since
that suggests linearity that doesn't feel quite right. And my own grief
space of divorce was far from Job-like in its proportions, but it is the
measure of liminality that I know and can try to describe. I am not
there now, I am elsewhere, and I have learned things I can't coherent-
ly express, and I am different in ways that are difficult to gauge. I can
move and breathe now, I have even fallen in love again, though differ-
ently—I'm more gun-shy, less enmeshed—the embrace feels wondrous
though sometimes foreign, the way joy after disappointment is not
exactly what it was in its first native form. I have a more present-tense
life now, less of the reflective impulse that I used to have probably as
a result of an old-fashioned childhood with a milk cow instead of the
Sega Genesis or dial-up internet of other kids in the eighties and nine-
ties. And also less of a planning impulse. I used to list goals for the year
that would produce, I felt, the kind of person I desired to be, someone
who would go to Greece before age thirty, would learn banjo and not
something boring like piano, would garden in raised beds—lists written
with careful casual messiness and stuck on the fridge to remind me of
how to achieve a life that would be approved of, applauded. My husband was part of this; we mutually imagined our selves into some wildly
beautiful people. And on a list more private I wrote the goal of a baby
and how we would leave Oregon where we lived most of our married
life and move to West Virginia and the baby would become a little
girl on a blue bike, in a little dress flapping, some streamers from the
handlebars rippling as she'd ride up that stretch of road past the cattle guard to meet my mother, lilacs infusing the air everyplace around
them both with a damp scent, and the girl, my girl, would exist in that
contained bowl of a world that I was once held by. Anyway, then there
was the divorce, and so the question of a child, along with the other
items on the long list, moved someplace out of my reach.

There are other differences. People seem less knowable, more frac-
tured. So does God. I worry sometimes that connections, when fully
exposed, can only be superficial and selfish, and freedom in unmarried-
ness only isolating. I worry that cleverness is replacing wisdom in what
I read because I struggle to believe in wisdom, collegiality replacing
friendship because I jettisoned many old friendships that seemed to belong to a different self, mild appetite replacing hunger because hunger

is too frightening in its insatiability, and reason or practicality replacing blind faith because I don't feel blind. And there is the strange forgetting, too: the way you begin to forget the textures of your marriage so that the first time it snows in your new life and the world goes white you sense that the same quietly disastrous thing is happening to your memory and you hope maybe that means you're not as shallow and strange as you fear because snow only conceals, does not obliterate— surely somewhere the intensity of relation and connection still resides in you even though your days sometimes have a pallor, a vagueness.

Some stay at that threshold an awfully long time, like my friend whose father has Alzheimer's and cries each time she leaves him, like those living with abuse, with chronic pain, with the threat of beheading or torture or paralysis. Some lives are indeed Book-of-Job-like. People bear all sorts of unbearable things. I know I am fortunate to have gone to a place that felt impossible only once in my life so far—that place of alarm and estrangement from the self.

Some end the painful liminal hovering by suicide. But for most of us, the moving on with life is predictable; most people don't stay there, perhaps just because of tiredness and time—give it a year, they all said to me because most of them knew, most of them had had such a year themselves. Who knows what pulls us out of it really? It could be neglect, or forgiveness. I read in a self-help book that says forgiveness means seeing the childhood hurts that have hardened someone, seeing the panorama of the person and not just the fuckup. And maybe it did help me to see my husband as a kid napping or on his bike, and seeing myself too, also as more than a fuckup, as an open-hearted little girl belonging to her life.

Maybe it was God's Spirit, God's hand that pulled me out—some would say so. That image of my father possibly enfolding the heifer in his arms and lifting her out of her predicament, that's a nice image and evokes the Christ cradling the lost lamb that you see in paintings. But the truth is I can't say why I'm not there, any more definitively than I can say how we freed the Guernsey heifer from the iron ruts without her leg splintering.

After awhile you just become a divorced person, and the odor of tragedy fades from your life. Friends don't sniff at it every time they call, the wound of holidays and anniversaries and memory-infused objects goes unremarked, wedding-gift kitchen appliances become practical, your family plans Christmas. People expect things of you again—to chip in on your cousin's baby shower gift, to render the spiritual gleanings from divorce into comprehensible lessons of God's comfort and faithfulness. Your girlfriends announce their engagements and discuss their wedding plans without furtively checking your face for how you're taking it. You become a thirty-five-year-old academic with a dog but no children, cognizant, when you lift your head from grading essays, that your mother, now married for forty-plus years, had four children by the time she was your age.

How we get from there to here is maybe not the interesting thing.

The interesting thing is the nostalgia for the heartache. How you miss it.

How, when you study that image of the calf caught in the cattle guard, you see the alarm in her eyes, yes, but also the surprise felt in finding her body in such a state, finding that she in fact has no control, she is merely here in brilliant pain that clarifies she is alive. For me, in that liminal state, a kind of chemical change transmuted my striving and my conscious self-shaping and my perfectionism into breakage, and the whole pulsing ache was the most honest prayer I've ever been able to pray. At the threshold, I had for the first time a sharp sense of being somehow loved in the midst of failure. Then, after a time, you're not there anymore. You begin to know yourself after the event of estrangement—responsible and capable again, you can meet deadlines, you can have a relationship with a man again, in real friendship, you are not ruined for intimacy. You can shop for your own groceries and eat meals again like a normal person because life has become possible and level. You are relieved that that's all over, you are content even. So you have difficulty understanding why on earth, at an unguarded moment, you grow suddenly desperate for that bright pain to return. You cannot understand why you miss the astringent air, why you long for the harsh naked bawling to come from your animal throat.

JESSIE VAN EERDEN'S novel, *Glorybound*, won the 2012 Foreword Reviews' Editor's Choice Fiction Prize. Her second novel, *My Radio Radio*, is forthcoming with Vandalia Press, WVU Press's fiction imprint, this spring. Her work has appeared in *The Oxford American*, *Bellingham Review*, *The River Teeth Reader*, *Best American Spiritual Writing*, along with two recent Appalachian anthologies: *Red Holler* and *Walk Till the Dogs Get Mean*. She received her MFA in nonfiction writing at the University of Iowa, and was awarded the 2007-2008 Milton Fellowship at *Image* and Seattle Pacific University for work on *Glorybound*. She directs the low-residency MFA writing program at West Virginia Wesleyan College.

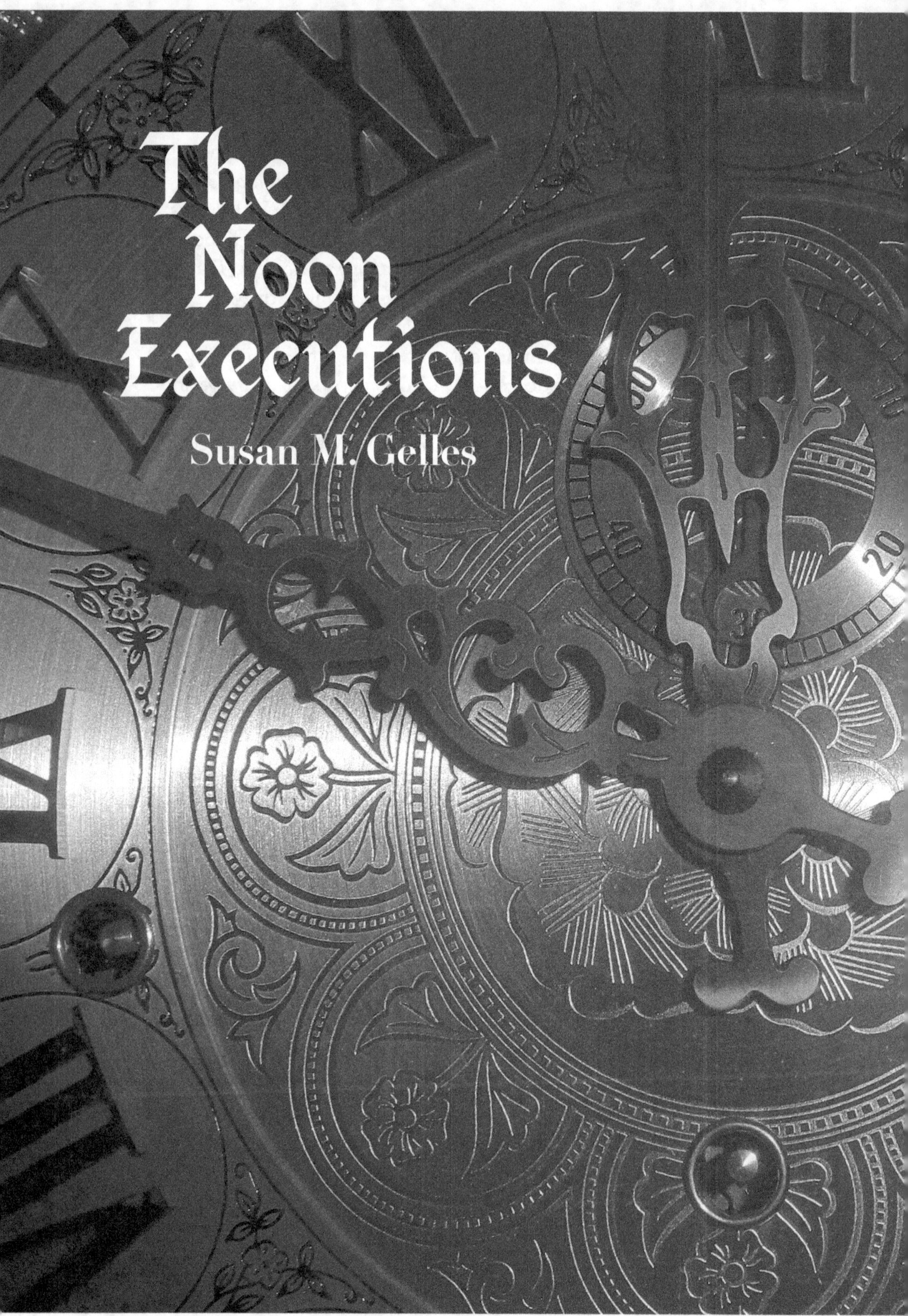

The
Noon
Executions
Susan M. Gelles

The general had chosen him because everyone said he had beautiful handwriting: the clearest and yet most ornate in all the three towns. For ten years, he'd written the baptismal and marriage certificates for the Church of Santa Teresa; he'd even painted the borders of these documents with a brush made from the hair of an ox. Now he sat behind a desk at the jail, in a room that somehow remained cool despite the summer heat, as one by one the condemned shuffled in and sank on the unyielding chair before him. Those who could not walk were dragged by soldiers, but in all cases their escorts left them alone with Antonio. The guards preferred to stand outside the door and observe the buzz of the large anteroom.

When he first assumed the role of state calligrapher, Antonio mostly gaped at the slumped figures. They were brought to the jail each night, crammed into small trucks. Some soldiers claimed the prisoners were dangerous revolutionaries from the far-off western coast. Others stated, with equal authority, that the prisoners were criminals who had hidden in the mountains. Antonio could, perhaps, have determined the truth, but the list of approved questions for interrogation did not cover place of origin.

> **[H]e would find himself staring at the prisoners, who themselves mostly gazed at the floor's wide planks. I am not like them, thought Antonio.**

For the first three days of the noon executions, Antonio did not ask the prisoners anything at all. He sat behind his desk, fiddling with the sleek black pen that was much smarter than the worn brushes he'd used for church documents. He tried to look everywhere but at whichever man sat before him. The calligrapher watched the clock on the wall swing a copper pendulum back and forth. He tried to appreciate the yellow sunlight that bathed the room and which made it irrelevant that here, as in all the towns, the electricity could not be relied upon. Inevitably, however, he would find himself staring at the prisoners, who themselves mostly gazed at the floor's wide planks. I am not like them, thought Antonio. They sought trouble, but I live in the same house in which I grew up, and I bother no one. I do not ask: what lies across the sea; or how may I find the treasures hidden in the tombs of kings. I do not ask: what if.

But because Antonio only stared at the prisoners and admired the clean shape of his pen, he failed to ask the requisite questions. Then at night he had to invent answers in his home, a four-room wooden shack that rested upon high stilts about a mile outside the town that held the jail. He willed his candle not to expire until he had conjured up the names of parents and spouses and children, varieties of occupation, and reasons for betraying the state. He knew no one would discover the falsity of what he wrote: the purpose of his records was not to provide clues for further arrests, which occurred according to a pattern known only to those in charge. Instead, as the general rather impressively explained, the red, leather-bound volume Antonio filled with his beautiful handwriting would one day go on permanent display inside a glass case at the museum. Future generations, said the general, would admire the state's perfect marriage of discipline and art.

To avoid losing sleep to invention, Antonio resolved to place the burden of revelation on those whom the state had chosen to bear it. Thus, on the fourth day of the noon executions, as the first enemy collapsed onto the empty chair, Antonio picked up his pen and said, firmly, "Name."

"José Santiago," was the faint reply.

"Age."

"Thirty-four."

"Occupation."

José Santiago lifted his head and smiled a little through broken teeth. "Cynic."

Antonio glanced at him, noted the man's bare feet, and wrote, "Shoemaker." Then he said, "Parents."

"None."

"Spouse."

José Santiago chortled. "None."

"Children."

The prisoner wiped his mouth. "None."

Antonio turned the page. "Reasons for betraying the state."

José Santiago said nothing.

"Reasons for betraying the state." said Antonio again, somewhat louder. José Santiago sighed and looked out the window, but it showed only the dusty courtyard where, in a few hours, he and two dozen other men would be shot. "There is no state," he said.

Antonio wrote, "Prisoner was recruited by an opposition party." The exchange seemed unsatisfactory. He was allotted twenty minutes per prisoner; scarcely ten minutes had passed, and José Santiago, staring at him, clearly expected something more.

The prisoner spoke and interrupted his thoughts. "What's your name?" asked José Santiago in a tone of some amusement.

Briefly Antonio worried that he might get in trouble if he answered, but he reassured himself that no harm could derive from altering the script with a man soon dead. "Antonio Sánchez."

"Age?"

"Thirty."

"Occupation?"

"Calligrapher."

"Parents?"

Antonio placed his pen on the desk at a neat right angle to the ledger.

"Parents?"

The calligrapher ran a finger along the gold-rimmed edge of the open page. "Dead," he said.

"Of course," said the prisoner. "Spouse? Is she dead, too?"

Antonio thought of María del Río, whom he had never even kissed. He remembered the curve of her hips; the solid thighs revealed when she raised her dress as she danced. His friends said she'd asked about him, that she wanted to know why he sat alone with his beer when everyone else danced and sang to celebrate victory. "We told her you don't know how to dance, that you can't sing," his friends had said, "and she claimed she'd teach you!"

"No spouse?" asked José Santiago.

"No."

"And childless."

"Correct."

José Santiago swayed; he half-turned and grasped the back of his chair. "Reasons for betraying the state?"

Antonio frowned.

"Reasons for—"

"Next!" called the calligrapher. The door swung open, and two young soldiers dragged José Santiago back to the holding pen to await the next round of executions.

Later, Antonio ate lunch at his desk and, as usual, kept his back to the window as feet scuffled across the courtyard. He waited, flinched at the loud crackle of guns, and then resumed his meal amid the sound of cheers. At precisely one o'clock, he called for the next prisoner.

A single guard hurried in, pushing a middle-aged man before him. The prisoner, not as battered as many of the others, seated himself as the guard closed the door.

"Name," said Antonio.

"My name is Luís Rivera, Antonio Sánchez."

> 'We know you,' said Luís Rivera. 'Before he died, José Santiago told the rest of us what he'd learned.'

Antonio looked up sharply. The prisoner wore a mustard-colored jacket, a dirty white shirt, and olive-green trousers; his face, with its hooded eyes and thick moustache, was unfamiliar.

"Do I know you?" asked Antonio.

"We know you," said Luís Rivera. "Before he died, José Santiago told the rest of us what he'd learned."

Silently, Antonio reproached himself for departing from official policy. But he knew of no actual prohibition against telling a prisoner his name or other such insignificant details. And the prisoners couldn't harm him.

"Age," said Antonio Sánchez.

"Forty-five."

"Occupation."

"I'm not as talented as you, I'm afraid." The prisoner leaned forward a little to better view the open volume on Antonio's desk. "I do find your calligraphy quite impressive."

"Occupation."

Luís Rivera seemed to consider. "Thief," he said, primly folding his hands.

Antonio hesitated, but then wrote "thief" in his beautiful, looping script. "Parents?"

"Dead," said the prisoner cheerfully.

"Spouse?"

"She's a rather private individual, and I neglected her shamefully. Perhaps just say I'm not married."

"Ana Rivera," wrote Antonio, borrowing the first name of one of his many cousins. "Children?" he asked.

"A disappointment. The eldest is secretary to the general. At least he had the good sense to use a false name."

"None," wrote Antonio. He'd arrived at the question he hated most. "Reasons for betraying the state?"

"Well," said Luís Rivera. "Where to begin."

Antonio waited, but the prisoner seemed to have forgotten him. "Reasons for—"

"Yes, yes," Luís Rivera said. "Well. Boredom, really. Treason promised a great deal of excitement. Plus," he sighed, "the general's wife is quite exquisite."

> # "They never repeated a question, leading him to suspect they had agreed among themselves what each would ask."

Antonio frowned at him; the prisoner gazed complacently back. The calligrapher picked up his pen and wrote, "Denies everything." The ledger was to reflect the execution only of confessed criminals, but surely no one would ever inspect page forty-seven out of a nine hundred page book.

"And now I have some questions for you," said Luís Rivera. "Favorite color?"

Antonio put down his pen. "Orange."

"Favorite poet?"

"I don't read poetry."

"Ah, but you should. I particularly recommend the love poetry of the last century." The prisoner brushed some invisible lint from his sleeve. "And finally, share with me a memory of your boyhood. Tell me something you did when you were ten."

"I had no boyhood."

"Now, now. We just want a mere scrap of information. Climb any palm trees? Feed any chickens?"

"We?"

"It gets very dull down in the holding pen. Why, if you were to tell me about pulling a girl's pigtails, it would probably entertain us for a clear half hour."

Antonio pushed back his chair from his desk.

"How about age twelve?" persisted the prisoner.

"I left school at age twelve."

"Really! But you write so beautifully."

The calligrapher rose and shouted, "Next!" Instantly, the door opened, and a soldier pulled the prisoner from the room.

"A pleasure!" called Luís Rivera.

For the rest of the afternoon, each of the condemned men asked Antonio about himself. They never repeated a question, leading him to suspect they had agreed among themselves what each would ask. He searched for a purpose in their interrogation, but they never asked anything that could help them. By the end of the day, the prisoners had learned only trivia: that as a boy, he'd been fond of a white goat named Lucy; that his earliest memory was of peering through the gray netting that hung over his bed; that at night he prayed to the Blessed Virgin. He weighed one-hundred-forty pounds. His father had had blue eyes. By evening he felt unsettled, certain the prisoners were draining him of life through imperceptible drops. He stopped at the bar on his way home and drank his beer in a corner. The bar's electric lights, though flickering, always jolted him into a sullen wakefulness. "Dance, Antonio!" urged his friends. They stomped in a line, one man's hands upon the shoulders of the next, as María del Río sat on top of the piano and clapped.

The next day, the crows that pecked at unpromising dirt outside of the jail scattered as Antonio approached. Once inside, he found soldiers talking excitedly in the anteroom.

"Did you hear?" asked a stocky guard named Miguel Carrera.

"Hear what?" asked Antonio.

"Six prisoners tunneled out at midnight."

"How?"

"They may have had help on the inside." Miguel beamed, and Antonio thought he knew why: the execution of a few senior guards could easily result in a promotion for the young soldier. "They're somewhere in the forest," Miguel continued. "Maybe heading for the coast. We'll catch them, of course."

"Of course." Antonio cupped the cool metal doorknob of his office. "Why only six?"

Miguel shrugged. "Some would rather die here than be shot in the forest and eaten by dogs. And some hoped for clemency by staying."

"Will they get clemency?"

Miguel laughed heartily and slapped a fellow soldier on the back as an introduction to the story of the naïve calligrapher.

Antonio slipped into his office and sat down. He paused for a moment, as he did every morning, to sniff the air. He smelled wood dust, and something he wished were chalk, as in a schoolroom, but which instead suggested only an indefinite staleness. He fingered his slender pen and imagined that it held him aloft, sleeping upon a cloud.

He turned the ledger's pages: Luís Rivera, Hector López, Pablo Aguilar, Guillermo Martínez. These men, perhaps, were now crawling through brush, wading through streams, but really they weren't free at all, because they were running away, and there would always be something to run away from, and that something would never halt the chase. The regime's reach was wide; everyone knew stories of people knifed on the street, or found dead beneath bridges, even across oceans in faraway cities where they must have thought: here I am safe; here I may rest. Better, thought Antonio, to remain in one place; to scratch ink upon a page; to ask only what is permitted and then not care about the answers.

But he could not resist questioning a prisoner about the previous night's escape and whether, in particular, Luís Rivera had fled or remained.

"He was the first to climb down the hole," said the prisoner, a short, bald man who held his broken arm against his chest.

Antonio thought of Luís Rivera and his jaunty air and felt, somehow, fooled.

"He told us you would ask about him," continued the prisoner. "He left you a message."

The calligrapher waited, but the man said nothing.

"Well?" asked Antonio.

"He said," the prisoner lowered his voice confidentially, "that a man who loves both the color orange and the Blessed Virgin need not be lost. And he said he hoped to see you again."

"He's dead," said Antonio, picking up his pen.

"No. Luís Rivera has powerful friends. He escaped. He won't die."

"Name," said Antonio.

> # "His life seemed filled with the incessant murmur of other men's voices, and those voices paused only for the awful punctuation of guns."

The days blurred together. The first week of the noon executions passed, and the second began. Antonio, flipping through the ledger, could not match names to faces. In the evenings, as he walked past the wilting mango trees, he sometimes thought he heard in the croaking of frogs a note of rebuke. Once or twice he sensed a purposeful rustle amid the tall grasses, but he sped up at such times, and no one ever appeared. As he lay in bed, he tried to pray to the Mother of God, but he feared she couldn't hear him. His life seemed filled with the incessant murmur of other men's voices, and those voices paused only for the awful punctuation of guns.

Toward the end of the second week of the noon executions, as the calligrapher arrived for the day's interviews, the soldier Miguel called to him.

"Did you hear? The general's wife has run away."

"To where?" Already Antonio found it easy to forget the world held more than his home, the bar, and the jail.

"Straight into the arms of another man."

"Who would dare?"

"They'll catch him," said Miguel. "Then it will get interesting around here. That interview, I'll attend!"

On Saturday evening, Antonio sat in his customary seat in the bar's darkest corner. The crowd sang of victory and of love. Suddenly the pianist, a quick-witted man, stopped playing. The general and two of his officers entered the bar.

Everyone stood up. The general, reputed to be rather easygoing despite his high rank, made a gesture, and everyone sat down. At a nod from one of the officers, the pianist commenced a lively tune.

The crowd shuddered with a tentative relief. Drinks were poured; laughter bubbled through the room. A man pulled his girlfriend on to the dance floor, and other couples joined them. María del Río stood and chatted with the pianist, occasionally displaying a fine row of white teeth.

Antonio saw the general say something to an officer, who then brought María del Río to the general's table. She accepted a glass of beer.

The calligrapher strained to listen.

"You're a beautiful woman," said the general.

"Thank you. But not everyone thinks so."

"Impossible."

María arched a lovely eyebrow. "Sitting behind you is a man who would rather drink alone than dance with me."

The general turned; Antonio hastily gulped his beer.

"I'll have him arrested," said the general.

Antonio's stomach tightened. But then the sound of María's laugh reminded him of pennies landing in a jar, and somehow, inexplicably, he relaxed a little.

"No," she said. "He's only stupid. He isn't," her eyes traveled over the general's uniform, "distinguished."

"For some women," said the general, "distinction isn't enough."

"Mmm," said María. She gazed adoringly at his large ears, his jowls, his graying hair. "I'm not some women."

"Let's dance," said the general.

Antonio watched the general's large red hands caress María's body. They danced closely together, María whispering in his ear.

One of Antonio's friends, Pedro López, drifted over to him.

"You missed your chance," Pedro said.

"I had no chance."

"Just promise me that tonight of all nights, when we close with the song celebrating the regime, you join in. Maybe even look a little enthusiastic."

"I can't sing."

"Mouth the words."

But Antonio decided not to stay until the end. He left hurriedly, pressing himself against the wall, hoping not to be noticed. Outside a thousand stars filled the sky. As the bar's door closed, the crowd's noise converted to a dull murmur, and he again heard the voices of the condemned whispering their names, lying about the existence of wives and children, as though disclosure mattered, as though it could change a thing. He himself continued to answer the prisoners' frivolous questions quite honestly, for what did it matter if anyone knew that his father had cut sugar cane, or that his mother had salved his bee stings with mud to extract the venom? The details of one person's life and another person's life were interchangeable; he would be Antonio Sánchez even if his father had raised pigs instead of swinging a machete. He would be alone even if the general had not danced with Maria.

The third week of the noon executions began. Antonio felt weary; almost two hundred pages of the ledger were covered in his script. He wondered how long the noon executions would last: surely the regime could not pluck every man from his bed and shoot him? But then something terrible happened.

Antonio was questioning a prisoner when he heard a commotion in the anteroom.

"Idiots!" a man shouted. "Idiots!"

The calligrapher opened his office door a crack and peeped out.

The general was shaking first one guard and then another by the shoulders. "You had him here, and you let him escape! Is this a playground? Are you not soldiers of the regime?" He looked about as soldiers ducked into closets and hid behind one another. "Where are the records?" he demanded. "Who interviewed the man?"

Miguel Carrera stepped forward. "The calligrapher spoke with Luís Rivera."

"I don't want to hear the man's name!" shouted the general. "Where are the records?"

As in a dream, Antonio Sánchez fully opened his door. The general blustered into the office, sat behind the desk, and grabbed the ledger. He turned the pages with a kind of slap.

"Where," said the general, in a quiet, even tone that frightened the calligrapher more than the shouting, "are the records of"—here the general trembled—"the creature who seduced my wife?"

In a hollow voice, Antonio Sánchez said, "Page forty-seven."

The general read the forty-seventh page of the calligrapher's clear and beautiful handwriting.

"Did you write this?" said the general, tracing the letters with his beefy fingers.

"Yes, sir."

"All of it?"

"Yes, sir."

The general continued to stroke the page. "'Denies everything,'" he read aloud. "Why did you not record the man's reasons for betraying the state?"

Antonio opened his mouth, but no sound came.

"All of our criminals confess. Are you a propagandist?" The general rose and surveyed the calligrapher. His eyes narrowed. "Ah," he said softly. "The man who won't sing of victory, who won't dance. Well," and his voice hardened, "we'll see you dance tomorrow. Arrest this man!"

Two guards rushed into the office and seized Antonio by the arms. Miguel Carrera poked his head in to watch.

"You there," said the general to Miguel. "Interrogate the prisoners."

Miguel froze. Antonio knew the guard was wondering whether to consider this a promotion. Perhaps it was, for now Miguel would get to sit all day.

"Keep records," the general said. "Be thorough."

The guards dragged Antonio across the anteroom, through a small door, and down a flight of winding stairs. They flung him on the dirt floor and climbed back up. The door closed firmly behind them.

Slowly Antonio raised himself. Here and there, in the deepest shadows, sat perhaps two dozen men, ragged and bruised. Some men's eyes were closed, so that he couldn't tell if they were sleeping or dead.

"Welcome, Antonio Sánchez," said a gaunt figure.

The calligrapher recognized the speaker; he had interviewed the man only an hour earlier. Already he'd forgotten everything about him.

"I'm sorry," began Antonio by way of asking the prisoner to repeat his name, but the man waved his hand.

"You are to die tomorrow," the prisoner said.

Antonio wondered if he were expected to agree, but he refused to accept that he was himself condemned. There was the matter of his handwriting, the most beautiful in all the three towns. Miguel would scribble like the footprints of a peacock. The museum needed Antonio's art. The red-leather volume was unfinished.

"Who will remember you?" asked the gaunt prisoner.

Antonio sank to his knees: suddenly the room felt close and hot. He wiped his brow.

"Your parents are dead," the prisoner intoned, as though this was a chant he had learned and was reciting now as a requiem. "You have no spouse, no children. Your brothers and sisters are long lost. In a few hours, your friends will deny ever having known you. Who remembers you even at this moment?"

The calligrapher thought of all those baptismal and marriage certificates for the Church of Santa Teresa, but he'd penned them in the quiet of his room, and they were all unsigned. Even the nine-hundred-page ledger contained details only of other men's lives.

"You were kind to us," said the prisoner.

"Kind?" asked Antonio.

"You didn't beat us."

Antonio remembered the general's instruction to Miguel: "Be thorough." But it had never occurred to the calligrapher to beat anyone.

"You didn't force us," the prisoner continued, "to reveal the names of our families."

'Here is a story,' said the prisoner soothingly. 'There once lived a boy named Antonio Sanchez.'

Some of the other men murmured an approval.

"But who will remember you?" asked the prisoner again.

Antonio looked around him. Some of the men he vaguely recognized; others, he'd never met. The gray walls against which they rested glistened with damp. He became aware of a sour stench. No one left here except to confess and to die.

He felt dizzy and reached for the floor to steady himself.

"We knew you'd join us," said the prisoner a little sadly. "Luís Rivera said so. He said you were too good to stay out of trouble for long."

"I wasn't good," said Antonio. "I was sloppy."

"Good; sloppy. Does it matter? You left us alone, and yet you listened. A rare gift."

Antonio lay on the hard dirt and gazed at the brown rafters of the ceiling far above.

"Here is a story," said the prisoner soothingly. "There once lived a boy named Antonio Sánchez. His mother's name was Carmen; his father's name was Ricardo. His father had eyes the color of the summer sky. His mother kept her long hair piled on her head in a brown scarf. Every year, on the night before the Feast of the Three Kings, the boy would put under his bed a handful of grass for the Wise Men's camels. In the morning, the grass would be gone, and the boy would find an orange candy and three pennies."

Antonio began to weep.

The gaunt prisoner's voice droned on, and when it faltered, another prisoner took up the tale, and then another. The calligrapher's life spun out before him, and a thousand inconsequential details became one whole. He heard the story of a lonely man who prayed but did not believe he could be heard. Yet the condemned assured him that someone had listened and, for a little while, until noon the next day, would remember.

In the morning, two guards hustled him up to his old office. Miguel sat behind the desk and nodded pleasantly.

"Name? I know the answer, but I have to ask. Rules, you know."

"Antonio Sánchez." The calligrapher eased himself into a chair and saw that Miguel's writing was indeed an illegible mess.

"Age?"

"Thirty."

"Occupation?"

"Calligrapher."

"Parents?"

"Dead."

"Spouse?"

"None; children also none."

Miguel glanced up at him, then scribbled for a moment longer.

"Reasons for betraying the state?"

The infamous question, but Antonio Sánchez had failed to invent an answer for it.

"Reasons for betraying the state?"

The calligrapher thought. "How about—inattention to detail?"

Miguel frowned and wrote something that seemed too long to reflect Antonio's words. The calligrapher felt emboldened.

"Miguel," he said gently, "what is your favorite color?"

The soldier stared at him. "Green. Why do you ask?"

Antonio shrugged. "Maybe it will matter someday."

"I don't see how. Well, take care. I hear it's all over very fast. Next!"

At two minutes to noon, guards dragged Antonio and two dozen other men across the courtyard. The calligrapher's hands were tied behind his back. He declined the offer of a blindfold and glimpsed the office where, only yesterday, he'd been eating his lunch at just this time.

Facing him were twelve guards holding rifles. Who are they? he wondered. Do they know how soon they will be pressed against this wall?

He said a quick prayer to the Blessed Virgin, and it seemed to him that this time she listened, for she answered with a thunderous roar.

SUSAN M. GELLES is currently an MFA student at Columbia University. She lives in the Bronx with her husband and children.

F. DANIEL RZICZNEK

F. Daniel Rzicznek is the author of two poetry collections, *Divination Machine* (Free Verse Editions/Parlor Press, 2009) and *Neck of the World* (Utah State University Press, 2007), as well as four chapbooks, most recently *Live Feeds* (Epiphany Editions, 2015). His poems have recently appeared or are forthcoming in *The Kenyon Review, Massachusetts Review, Drunken Boat, TYPO*, and *Forklift, Ohio*. Also coeditor of *The Rose Metal Press Field Guide to Prose Poetry: Contemporary Poets in Discussion and Practice* (Rose Metal Press, 2010), Rzicznek teaches writing at Bowling Green State University.

Palimpsest Erasure

car dealership, Wood County, Ohio

Whatever was once here drains
through the eyes of the waiting:

the old man wearing black dress socks
with shorts has been here

forever. Long before him animals
wore trails through oak thickets,

river-fed marshes, made names for
one another and never spoke them,

taught them to no one.
A young woman in Roman sandals

takes her place and human history
rewinds and restarts, unconvinced

of its own importance.
Small trees from two states away

gesture above freshly-spread mulch.
No roots hold me to this ground.

Hosta

Bumblebees hover into

and out of this temple
in the city of green shade

all morning, intent
on worship, on

their endless prayers of pollen.

Nature

One termite stomachs
an acre of plywood, ten

a continent of trim and flooring
drenched in decades of rain.

A hundred and they deify the house
as a mountain of powder.

Everything human in me
recoils at their appetite.

Everything human
really should know better.

Communal

Five crows in the grassplot
where a factory once loomed

extol their latest meal,
crying above my headphones.

We're here in this place together
and then swiftly in the past

though also not too far ahead—
a realization deep in the texture

of every over-employed metaphor,
the failings beginning to show

as the present moment progresses.
The clouds rust shut overhead,

the music's shivering pulse frays
on their din, their dusk ruckus.

I should have just kept walking.
The beauty was unapproachable.

Hubris

The promised age
was upon us. Satan,
famous for dandruff,
snowed into the hive:

breeze weaving in, out
of ovens, mail slots,
the view vivid with
gravel and soot, frost,

bird chatter and fog—
vivid with resurrections,
even the headless
and all the lost virgins,

the wrinkles, the scars.
Age of elasticity, of
etcetera, of mascara,
of salvation unmasked

at last as oppression,
of arrogance renewed
an act at a time, like
an exhale of altitude:

floods from very deep,
lakes unfolding clear,
old rivers being born,
pieces of the whole,

tree upon tree, world
after world. Found his
machinery by the river—
knew it all to be a ruse.

Cadillac Man

Eric Lloyd Blix

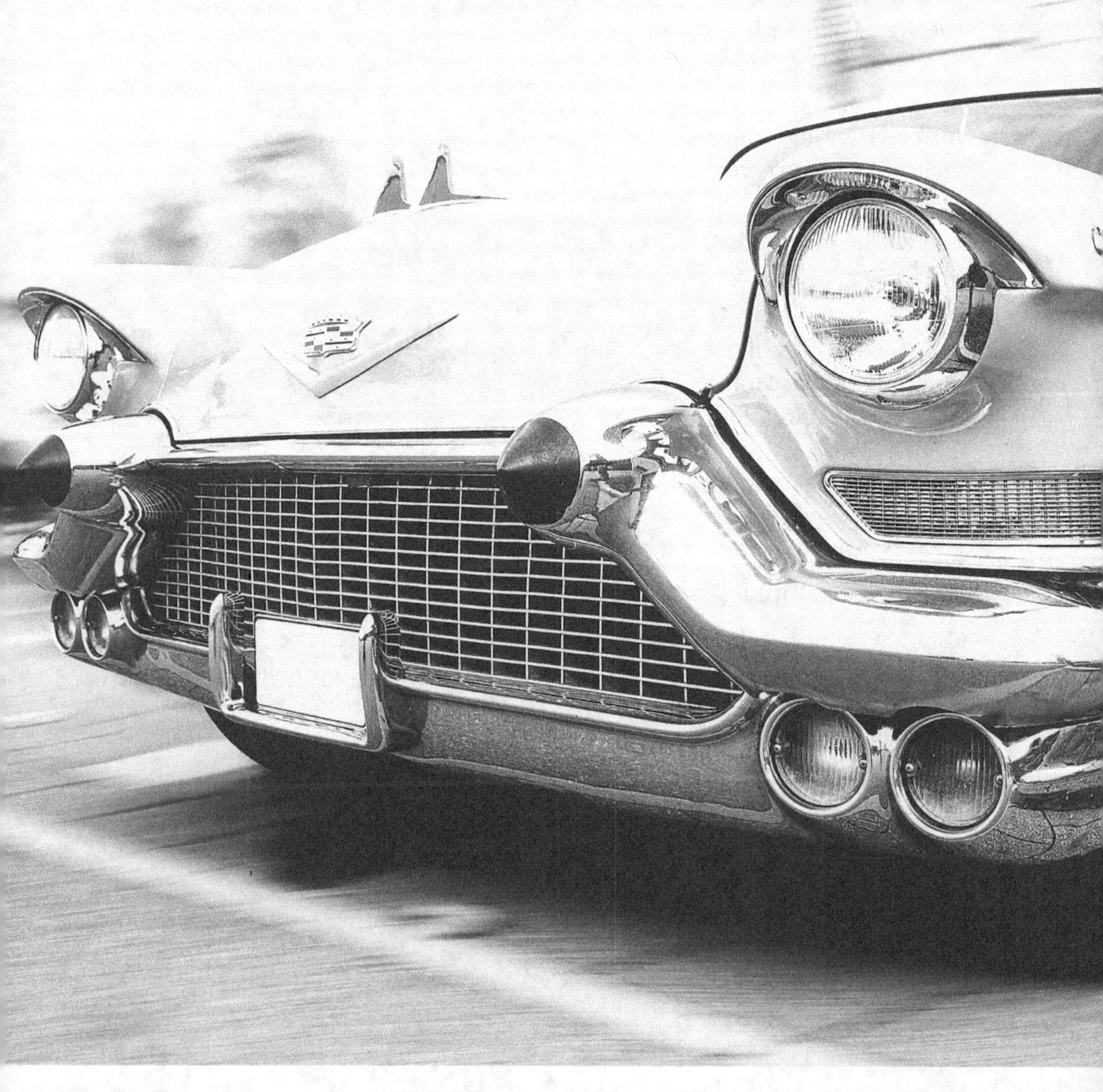

The swatch of dirt had not always been in the family. It was Indian land once, and before that, as Conrad Brady always says, it belonged only to the wildlife and the sacred maker. It was harnessed, subdued, and made tenable by the first who roamed it, then rediscovered and stolen and turned into something else entirely—a pioneer outpost, a dumping ground, an incinerator, a lot deemed vacant by the laws of private property—and now, under the Brady name a full century after the family obtained it, it's a scrap heap, tucked behind a Ford dealership and the Super Walmart.

The thruway skirts the edge of this diverse sector. The traffic to the west seems to underline old Conrad's voice when he says this kind of stuff about the frailty of their ownership, the blind luck that allows them to call this place theirs. The hum of various motor vehicles does not intrude upon him. Nor does it make his voice seem small. Not when he talks to his boy, Clint. Nor when he is alone, reminiscing about what he has.

This morning as he drives, Conrad Brady, in hushed murmurs, points out to no one but himself that despite their family's particular history on this parcel, the scrap yard which they have built on it belongs to them.

Every last inch.

He'll tell it this way to the journalist from Sioux Falls who is coming to visit this afternoon, mainly, Conrad supposes, to ask about the family's other luck, the ticket that made Conrad an even wealthier man, a copy of which hangs framed in the office he shares with the boy. But Conrad, a man of strong resolve, knows he won't lose focus. He'll tell this journalist how, on its centennial birthday, the other folks in Mankato still refer to the scrap yard by the Bradys' name, as in: I got a old washer I need taken to Brady's. When are you bringing that Yugo to Brady's—I got some shit I need to get rid of. Them Bradys are the people of junk and the scrap handling magnet.

And how by this—Brady—they mean the patch of earth.

They have meant it this way for decades.

Indian Jim makes footprints in the dirt and counts scrap, pile by pile.

He numbers the crushed washing machines.

He arranges the disembodied fenders in rows of two.

He gives names to the bundle of TV antennas tangled in the lot's corner, where the fence has been peeled back from its post by some anonymous being. Coyote, perhaps, or Spider. Some human thief.

This antenna is Wasp Removed From Nest. That one, Glistening Snake. And on top, Antler Without a Head.

None of this belongs to him.

He records his count on the receipts that Clint, the boy, the miserable boy as tall and cumbersome as a Sasquatch, gave him, to make sure nothing has gone missing. The receipts are clipped to a board and composed of three sheets each: a white one on top, then a yellow, then a pink, of which the latter two record his writings in faded imprints. His scrawls are messy. The blue pen is tiny between his wracked and swollen hands. He has turned many wrenches, dug many holes, broken

the teeth of many drunkards in his time. He is tall, though not as tall
as the boy; the heaps go just twice as high as Indian Jim stands. The old
man calls them crags, or gorges, or mountains. The old man calls them
extensions of the soil. The old man calls him Tonto or Sue, the lady's
name, in moments of anger and heightened intensity, or simply to make
fun. The old man brags about the Brady home, which he has named

"This antenna is Wasp Removed From Nest. That one, Glistening Snake. And on top, Antler Without a Head."

"Sod House." It rests in the wedge of dirt where the river bends north
like a crimped, useless pipe. The old man calls the river the Tigris and
Euphrates. The old man does not understand that of which he speaks.
The old man does not understand much.

Katie Gardner departs downtown Sioux Falls in the Ford Ranger
lent to her by the *Argus Ledger*. She coasts along the I-90 corridor
between towns that have stood for one hundred years or less. Between
them are short, grassy buttes and plains that flatten as she heads east.
Small towns whose economies are surprisingly robust. There's great
money in churning earth, in soaking it with confusing blends of fertiliz-
er and poison. Or, like the subject of her afternoon interview has done,
covering it with junk.

She passes through Brandon, Luverne, Worthington. At a stoplight
in Sherburn, she gets caught behind a brand new six-wheel Chevy that
rumbles along like a shiny waxed buffalo. She only notices because it is
so common. The driver turns off the main road and there is a different
truck in front of her, a gleaming Ford with a heavy steel winch fixed to
its rear bumper. In a field outside town, a team of combines cuts acres
of yellow wheat as if to erase it from the face of the earth. There are
signs posted in the ditch: *Freyr by Syngenta*.

Conrad pulls in and sees Indian Jim going around, marking receipts tarnished by wrinkles and rings from coffee mugs set on them.

He enters the office and throws down his keys.

"What's Tonto doing out there? Why ain't he on the scale?"

"I got him on a top to bottom count," Clint says. "Had a hole in the fence this morning where someone could've snuck in."

"You get it fixed?"

"Will later."

"What do you got Billy doing?"

"He's handling the magnet."

"Right now?"

"Yup."

"Just sitting in there?"

"Yup."

"Well what the fuck is there for him to move?" Conrad says. "Dipshit." He hobbles to the far wall and pours himself coffee. "Any other news? If not I think I'll wash up for my big interview." He loosens the strings of his bolo tie. The denim underside of his breast is already blotted with sweat, wet spotty arches strung like an archipelago, broken fragments dotting his torso.

"A man from Saint Peter called yesterday evening," Clint says. "Left us a message. He says he's got a Cadillac he wants to get rid of. Says it's like new. You want me to call him back?"

"What's he want to get rid of a new Cadillac for?" Conrad says.

"Don't know," Clint says, shrugging. His chair doesn't have armrests. He wouldn't fit if it did. "Hey, maybe depending on how nice it is, you could take the Caddy for yourself and I could have your truck? We'd each have a ride, then."

"Hell no," Conrad says. "You think this is a damn trading post? Is your skull that thick?" He unbuttons his shirt. "Go ahead," he says. "Give him a call." He picks up a handkerchief from the desk and wets it in the bathroom sink. He wipes his hands and chest, then his face. He reaches for the sack of Red Man in his back pocket and pinches a giant brown wad between his fingers and folds it inside his cheek. He dumps his coffee, which is from yesterday. He spits into the cup.

No one can guess how old Indian Jim is. When they ask about his tattoos, his answers surprise them.

The one on his shoulder is a face—Buffalo Bill's, the Old West gun show exhibitor, with his eyes X-ed out.

The wings of Thunderbird span the width of his back, lightning bolts shooting from its eyes.

On his forearm is the eagle perched atop the anchored globe from his days tromping jungle bush between Saigon and Hanoi. On the other forearm, etched after his discharge from the Marines, the encircled profile of a plains warrior, head dressed in a hand flashing hippie peace against a striped plane of black, yellow, white, and red: the logo of his A.I.M. brothers, who stood beside him at the second Wounded Knee.

"You were an adult back then?" people sometimes say.

"Yes."

"You don't look old enough. How long have you been around?"

"As long as I have been."

"How tall are you?"

"This tall."

"Are you as tall as Conrad's boy? What's his name?"

"No."

"What's that bird on your back?"

"Wakinyan."

"What's that mean?"

He stands before a pyramid of wooden TV sets with their screens smashed. There is an axle, too, and several aluminum ladders laid flat, rungs missing or sprung like broken guitar strings. He marks these items down. His jeans are caked in yellow dust. His black hair seals in heat. He used to have a TV like one of these. He's never had cable or a telephone or an internet connection. He watched networks on the antenna when he owned a TV. He hasn't seen a TV like this since he can remember. He reads his news in the paper each day. He turns to see if the old man or the boy are watching him from behind. There's no one left for him to go home to.

Katie Gardner arrives a little after ten o'clock. She parks the newspaper's pickup beside a brand new Silverado, pearly white, which must belong to the proprietor. The parking lot is gravel and is littered with potholes. There is a white sign on the fence with plain red lettering: *Brady Iron and Scrap.* She wonders how much money a scrap yard takes in annually, or in a single day, or the extent to which the lottery has affected Conrad Brady's life.

A group of men huddles beneath a shingled overhang near the gate. A potbellied dude, perhaps a local, in a plaid snap shirt and seed cap. Complexion specked with dirt. Beside him, a very tall man, towheaded, dressed in denim. The tall man's jeans are tucked into his boots. They each lean on different sides of a car, a Cadillac. It looks almost brand new. Another spoil of the state lottery, perhaps. An older fellow—the proprietor, certainly—steps out of the office and shouts at the towhead, "Got off her, you oaf. You'll fuck up her glimmer."

The towhead backs away and stands tall, tightening his fists, two globes hanging at his waist.

"What're you gonna do?" the old man says.

A Native approaches them and sets a clipboarded wad of papers on the ground, securing them with a stone.

Katie surveys the establishment. The scrap heaps loom. They cast shadows across the dirt. She joins the huddle. No one seems to notice.

The Native hops in the Cadillac and steers it onto the scale, a large steel platform with iron bumpers running along each side. Conrad Brady totters in small circles as the scale spits out the vehicle's weight on a slip of paper. He wheezes between mirthful chuckles, turning to Katie, thrusting a thumb back over his shoulder. He flicks his eyebrows up and down, perhaps to indicate his satisfaction with the great American automobile being taken in before them.

"It's ours now," the towhead grumbles. He crosses his arms. "Sure as shit."

They all watch as the Native pulls the Cadillac forward off the scale and parks it in the clearing where it will be elevated and moved. He gets out, lights a cigarette, and stands by himself near the end of the lot. A frumpy teenager works across the way in the cab of the scrap magnet. Maybe seventeen or eighteen years old, already quite obese. There's some kind of logo on his shirt. Hunting or racing, Katie thinks. It's obscured by the dirty glass of the magnet's cab. The boy wears a camouflage cap, the brim of which is curved almost into a complete circle. His hair sticks out around his ears like dry grass.

The machine's heavy arm swings directly above the Cadillac. The boy turns on the magnet, and various screws and spikes and other twisted bits get sucked up out of the dirt like a spill in reverse. The

Cadillac doesn't budge until the magnet warms up some. When this happens the vehicle trembles, and its wheels begin to lift and drop. The Cadillac looks like it's making a true effort to resist the force acting upon it from above, until soon it relents and it too gets lifted. There is a deep mechanical groan as the boy swings it to the side of the scrap yard and places it atop a mound of crushed objects, some of which appear to have been vehicles once, as well. Flattened headlights. Steel bumpers twisted and elongated like warm taffy.

Conrad spits.

"You're the journalist, I suppose," he shouts above the deep wail of the machine.

"That's right," she says. "You must be Conrad."

"In the flesh."

He grabs her shoulder and starts in on pride and history and whatnot as he points at the slow swinging Cadillac.

"It'll be crushed this afternoon, which is the thing," he shouts. "We ain't special because this place is fit for a Caddy. We're special because we can take a perfectly good one and crush it to smithereens, no questions asked. Been doing it this way for a hundred years."

"That's quite a long time," Katie says.

"That motherfucker," Conrad muses, "on top that mountain of shit, is pristine. Not sure why in the hell this yokel wants to get rid of her."

No one, including Katie, can deny the object's beauty, how it suppresses the many facets of its design. The blue paint, reminiscent of the sky's infinite archways, is a firmament in miniature. The car's old owner collects his check from the towhead and leaves. She watches the Native smoke, his back against the brick office. Conrad pulls Katie closer and says he would drive the thing home himself if it wasn't proper to turn the son of a bitch into a lustrous 2,500 pound brick.

Indian Jim is a highly skilled marksman. When he was a boy, his family lived in a one-room structure in the woods near the river with a potbelly stove and a single skinny window. He shared a mattress with his seven siblings and hunted chipmunks during the day with stones and a leather thong. He was the second-oldest child. His father would sit outside their home on a stump all day drinking corn alcohol distilled by other unemployed Indians. His mother died in the birth of the youngest child. Jim's father would tell his children that the government gave

Indians alcohol to ruin their bodies and break their collective spirit. An Indian couldn't stand up for himself if he was too drunk to balance. He said it was a great perversion that they depended on the U.S. government for income. He drank every single day. He drank so much that as an old man he was blind. Their tiny house was located on the edge of a grass field. The neighbors were all Indians and lived within sight. It was a mile or so outside of town. They called it the Rez even though it wasn't a reservation. Sioux weren't allowed to have one of those in Minnesota. The grass was always high and swayed in the wind. Jim's oldest brother, Norman, would shovel snow in the winter with pieces of bark he'd collected the previous spring. They had no phone lines or electricity or running water.

One day, when Jim was thirteen, a man from the police station came to the Rez to tell the children about law enforcement. This policeman said that he was one-sixteenth Chippewa. He explained how policemen were friends, and that if their dads ever drank too much and became violent, they should call the police for help. He brought two rifles with him, a .30-06 and a .22. He asked the kids how many of their dads kept guns in the house. Jim and Norman and the dozen or so other children raised

> "Jim did not become a police officer. He used his skills to shoot communists in Vietnam. He used them to blow out the knee of a federal marshal in South Dakota."

their hands. The policeman shook his head and expressed his regret that their fathers found the resources for alcohol and weaponry but couldn't manage to feed their own kids or give them all shoes. Later, the police officer set up a pyramid of tin cans and let the older boys shoot at them. Norman handled the .22 and hit two cans. Thomas

Jefferson Dirty Belly, a year younger than Norman and a year older than Jim, used the other rifle and missed the cans completely. Jim used the same rifle and plunked each can, the one on top, then the row of two in the middle, and finally the row of three on the dirt. He did not miss once. The policeman patted his head and gave him a toy badge. He told Jim there might be a future for him in law enforcement if he didn't turn into a drunk who sat on a stump all day.

Jim did not become a police officer. He used his skills to shoot communists in Vietnam. He used them to blow out the knee of a federal marshal in South Dakota, after which he hid in the woods for six days hunting chipmunks with rocks. He doesn't fire guns anymore. He lives in an efficiency apartment in the old German end of town. He has never once in his life imbibed.

The Cadillac pitches now in the wind. Its shadow grows long and short. Old Conrad doesn't fret. The thing is heavy. He sits back in his chair and listens to the classifieds on the radio. His concern, he tells the journalist, is with the various asking prices for unwanted items, particularly those which are metallic and heavy. The day's paper is spread across his lap. Several unladen trucks are lined up outside. Their drivers are anxious to leave. There is a stack of checks on the desk waiting to be signed.

"Why does the price matter?" the journalist says, referring to the classifieds. "Can't you just use your lottery money?"

"My Lotto cash? Shit. What kind of a way is that to run a business?" He leans over and spits a little brown bomb into the Folger's can beside his desk. "That's all for personal financing. My house and the like. My truck. I won't invest it in the business, except what I need to keep it going. Hell no." He dabs his forehead with the handkerchief. The boy comes out of the bathroom wiping his hands on his shirt. "Plus," Conrad says, "I gotta make sure this bonehead has something to live on after I kick the bucket. He's been here his whole life, yet he don't know a work order from his ass cheek."

Clint stops and lengthens his spine. His face melts into a profound scowl. "I know what a work order is," he says. "That's them, right there." He points to a stack of papers on the filing cabinet beside the door.

"Looky here," Conrad says. "You must be Adam, naming the shit he sees."

The boy's skin turns red as he runs a hand through his hair. He leans forward and pounds his fist on the old man's desk. He breathes deeply. His chest and shoulders heave. His eyes are streaked with rage.

Conrad leans back in his chair and looks at Katie. "See what I have to live with?" he says. "Temper tantrum after temper tantrum."

The journalist sets down her pen and scratches her neck. The boy's face scrunches. He begins to cry. "I gotta go fix the god damn fence," he whimpers. He wipes his nose with his sleeve. His forearm is slicked with snot and drool. He grabs a rubber mallet from the old man's desk and tromps outside, leaving the door open behind him.

"Moron," Conrad says. "Can't shut the door when the AC is on."

Katie Gardner clears her throat. Her skin has reddened, too. "So," she says, "you were saying you keep your lottery winnings separate from your business finances."

"God damn. Is that all you want to ask about is my Lotto winnings? The *Free Press* already did a story about it. Why don't you go dig that story up if it interests you so much?" He spits again. The journalist, hardly out of childhood it seems, with her flouncing hair and glistening eyes and rosy cheeks like the pictures of the Virgin hanging in church, recoils at the sound of the little splash.

"No sir," she says. "That's not all I'm interested in. Not by any means."

"Well shoot, then. Let me have it."

Katie Gardner, a field reporter in the fourth year of her career at the *Argus Ledger*, is in deep in the process of writing and publishing one of the most extensive recent series on the current state of Dakota tribal members. Her project is centered on the Pine Ridge Reservation, which serves as exemplar of the poverty and depletion of contemporary tribal life. In the previous year or so, she has filled three dozen notebooks with interview transcripts given to her by elders, men, women, and children, detailing their days spent studying the language, working as nurses, going to school, sitting around and drinking, eating cheese and peanut butter dispensed by government agencies, smoking cigarettes, looking at the sky, listening to the wind, watching ballgames on TV, drawing shapes in the dirt, tidying their houses. Katie has never been poor herself. She grew up in Sisseton and went to the state college in Brookings and got a job in Sioux Falls straight out of school. She feels confident that her student loans will be paid in full by the time she's thirty-two. She visits her parents sometimes on the weekends and on all major holidays. She drives a Prius with thirty-six thousand miles on the odometer.

She can explain neither to herself nor to Conrad Brady her interest in taking on such a project. Sometimes, when she's driving home in the early night from some assignment about a local sculptor or the opening of a new grocery store, she imagines that the cars transform into buffaloes, the streets into plains of swaying switchgrass. Sometimes there's someone out walking—an old lady becomes a scout or a fearful deserter. Her high school soccer coach was gung-ho about spirit and the curation of school traditions. "You didn't plant this field," he would say. "You didn't dig the well that gives you water." She removes these sayings from their context and chews on them the way Brady chews his Red Man. She finds herself frequently wondering if a person died on the place she stands, or if some holy ritual was performed there, or nothing so important, if she simply shares footsteps with a man or woman or child who roamed here centuries earlier.

'I'm interested,' she says, 'in the things we know about ourselves that we simply refuse to see. The stuff that gets lost through history...'

The project feels like the indulgence of her natural sense of wonder, she tells the proprietor. That being so near the site of the largest public execution in United States history—the 1862 hanging of thirty-eight Dakota after the infamous land grab and subsequent uprising—it only made sense to trace the origins of Pine Ridge. She'd already been to Saint Peter, Fort Ridgely, and New Ulm. She'd already visited the site of the execution, now called Reconciliation Park, beside Mankato's civic center. She'd already dug through archives, found the names of those tried, those pardoned, and those executed; those in charge, those on the peripheries, those whose names were included in some log for no other reason than miserable happenstance.

"I'm interested," she says, "in the things we know about ourselves that we simply refuse to see. The stuff that gets lost through history and churns up in places we don't expect to find them."

"Well," the old man says, "if you feel so damn guilty about things that happened a hundred doggone years ago, we got ourselves a Sioux right outside. Maybe he can make you a headdress to wear around if you say pretty please." He hooks his finger and fishes the plug of tobacco from his cheek and drops it in the can. He stands and retreats into the bathroom. He closes the door behind him.

Clint is now thirty-four years old and six-feet, ten-inches tall, a whole foot greater than his father. He is in the tall grass with a rubber mallet, banging the fence back into shape. He mutters about thieves, about the right he has to keep what's in the family. There is a space large enough for a man to fit his body through, but it is not big enough for Clint. The clanging echos of his mallet blend with the air rippling over the interstate. His hand swallows the handle. His straining skin is flecked with red. The shirt on his back strains at the seams. His knees creak and join his spine in a sorrowful chorus of pops. When he stands, his skeleton screams.

There is no breeze today, again. The whole summer has been windless. One long day in which the leaves and grass have not once flicked. The sun is very hot. The smell of the drainage ditch near the scrap yard lifts and percolates the afternoon. Clint can tell that the dank scent will be thick all evening like an impassable fog. Many suns aim their rays directly at his squint. He sweeps a glistening forearm across his glistening brow. His skin, like a pig's, glistens. All his inches glisten. He is surrounded by slop. His slop. His father's slop. His family's slop, there for him to roll around in. Somehow it has value. He has a stake in this buildup of junk, whether his father will say so or not.

Billy Morgan, a part-timer, strolls out of the scrap yard and winks at Clint. He gets in his Escort and drives away. It's just Clint left who can operate the magnet if need be, although he hates doing it because the cab is cramped and he has to leave the door open and let his legs hang out when he's running it, which is dangerous. He enters the lot to make sure the Indian isn't sitting down, maybe drawing circles or stick figures in the dirt, his legs crossed, long pipe exuding smoke, or banging some skin drum to bring rain. The Indian stares at a pile. Clint sees the Cadillac resting atop a mound of shit. Its shadow is long and bent and reminds him of a depressed person. He passes the Indian with steps he makes heavy. All his life he's been among these heaps of scrap, kept here as if he himself was a spare part. The Indian should count him, should feel his presence.

The notion arises within his gut to climb the mound. He braces his feet between the crushed bodies and heaves himself upward. He reaches the minor summit in two strides and rests his shoulder against the car. It's heavy. He touches its steel body and then his own body, much softer and full of nerves.

Across the way, the reporter walks to her truck and leaves.

He is not a spare part. He is not a fender or a hubcap or an empty trunk. God damn this place, he thinks, and all the shit kept within its walls, piling up year after year as if the moments themselves gather here. He leans harder against the vehicle, rocks back, and thrusts his body into the passenger door. God damn his father's profits. The Cadillac doesn't tumble immediately. He sweats through his blue shirt, leans back, and thrusts himself again. He screams. The car moans, softly and then louder, as the dual forces of gravity and Clint's weight act upon it, and it pitches further forward and is overtaken by its own weight, rolling over like a dead man.

> He thinks about the Cadillac as he gets in his Jeep Cherokee and turns the engine over, the same late 80s model he has been driving since the early 2000s.

Indian Jim punches his card. On it, the hours that have accrued are stamped. He leaves the inventory sheets in their clipboard and places them in a slot by the office door. He thinks about the Cadillac as he gets in his Jeep Cherokee and turns the engine over, the same late 80s model he has been driving since the early 2000s. The old man, whenever he sees Jim pull in, asks how the vehicle's Injun is running. The old man has locked himself away. The old man lingers here for long hours. The old man seems to always be home, whether at the scrap yard or Sod House, or anyplace else. The old man stakes a claim on this world.

Indian Jim's vehicle gets eleven miles per gallon. The engine burns a quart of oil every month. He drives along the main drag, past the Olive Garden, the Home Goods, and the city's mall. The radio is turned to the local news. There is a story about a group of families who lost their homes in the recession and lived in tents they pitched in a wooded area a mile or so south of town. They stayed there for nearly a year. The reporter is amazed that such a lifestyle could be maintained for more than a few days. This is followed by a weather report. More heat. More sun. Soon Jim sees a tall denim figure walking along the shoulder of the road. He slows to pick up the boy but is honked at by the truck behind him as the boy waves him along.

Indian Jim has three cans of chicken noodle soup and half a jar of peanut butter in the cabinet at home. He counted over 2,500 parts today to make sure none had left the Brady's lot. All the pieces were there, each one accounted for, and it was as if his numbering of things had reinvented the place, renewing the existence of that small world the old man holds sacred. The stoplight ahead burns red and he stops, shuts off the radio. The old man needs a name. Sleeping Bear. Wobbling Horse. Cadillac Man.

 **ERIC LLOYD BLIX'S** writing has appeared in such journals as *Western Humanities Review*, *Caketrain*, *3:AM* magazine, and others, and it has been reprinted at Longform.org. He teaches creative writing at Minnesota State University, Mankato.

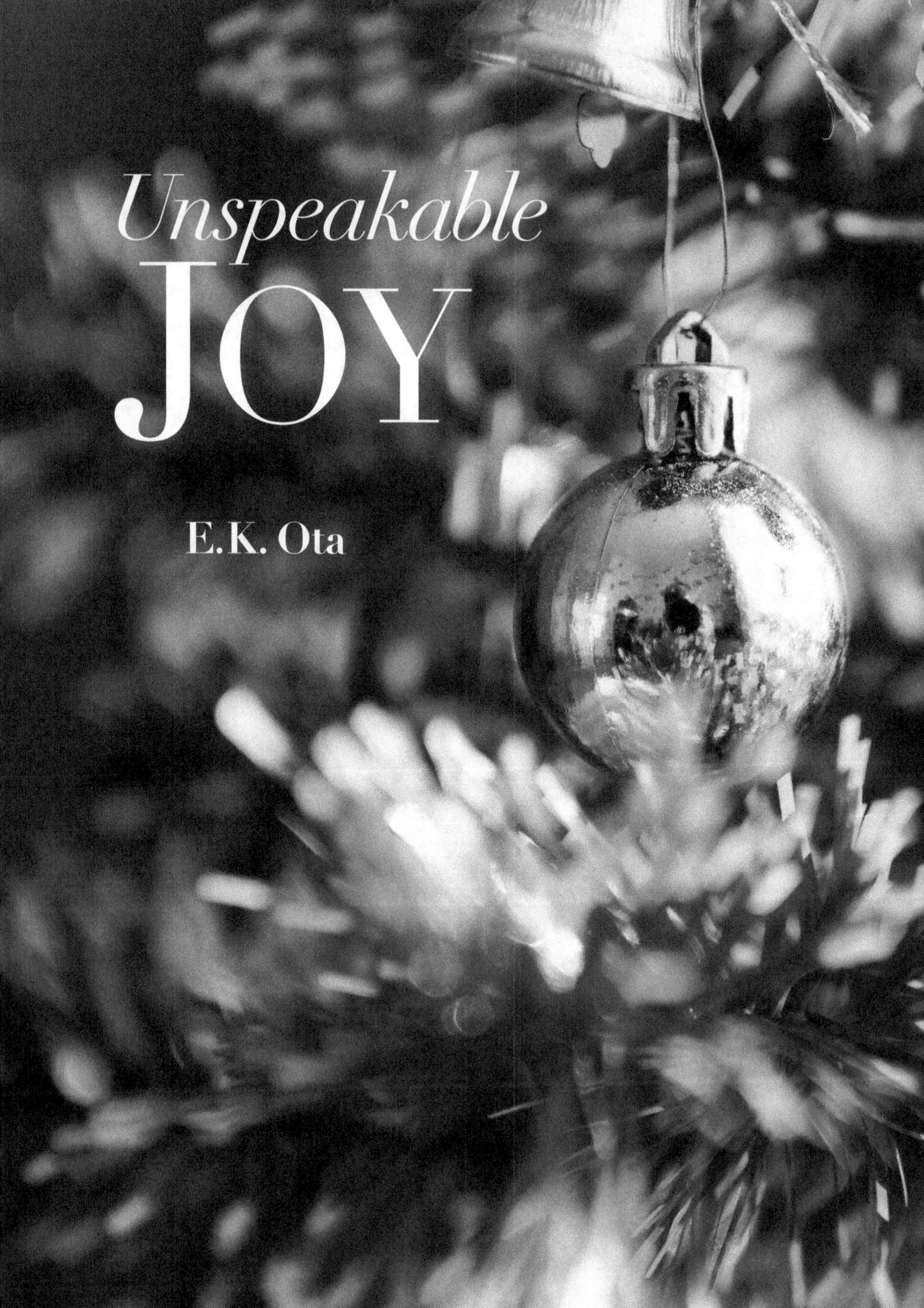

Unspeakable
JOY
E.K. Ota

The city caramelized around the dark hills, thinned into glittering rivulets along the highways. Like a phosphorescent web, a constellation of luminescent dew; there are moments when humanity can seem beautiful, thought Esther Kono, sitting next to the window. So beautiful. No matter how many times she saw the city at night from a plane, it always made her heart go still. Even now, after two stops and nine hours of flight, it made her heart go still. She breathed a spot of fog on the glass. And to think, just that morning she had been in Boston; she had left a house so old her landlord had a document warning her not to lick the paint; and now she was approaching Southern California; she was going home and it was Christmas.

The plane veered slightly to the left. She could no longer see the city. For a few moments they went gliding in the lucid, endless interstice between the heavens and the clouds, spread out like a soft grey cloth in all directions below—and then they descended. There was turbulence. The seatbelt icon overhead turned red with a *ping*. Throughout the cabin flickered a jolt of alarm. A baby in the front of the plane let out a cry. A woman in aisle eight placed a napkin to her lips, closed her eyes, and wished she had bought a bottle of Bacardi. At the back, strapped to a fold-down seat by the bathroom, the flight attendant sat unfazed; she thought of her lover—his hands, maple syrup, sunlight streaming through aluminum blinds.

In aisle fifteen, Esther prayed. Her prayers, which were long and effusive on the ground, were now short, breathless, clipped as Morse code. Dear God! Please. Not now. Please! Save us. She tried not to clutch the armrests and think of dying, then chided herself for being so afraid. She was a child of God. Death would be nothing but the portal to heaven, yet her faith was failing, slipping like vapor away.

> ## "Her prayers, which were long and effusive on the ground, were now short, breathless, clipped as Morse code."

The plane stabilized. Shoulders loosened with relief. Pressing her forehead against the glass, Esther sighed. How quickly she turned! How easily she lost her way. She thought of Isaac, who was still in Boston finishing up his final exams at seminary, and knew that he would not have been afraid. The night before, they had walked through the Common. The ground was white, bashful from the recent snowfall, and the black trees were strung up festively with Christmas lights. Isaac held her hand in his pocket because she had forgotten her mittens, and as they made a slow circuit of the park, they talked about marriage. In a week he would fly out to California to join her family for Christmas. When she turned towards him, there was snow in his hair, and she could tell that he was nervous. And what should I bring? Who will I meet? he had asked as they watched children ice skating in the park.

Isaac frowning in the snow, children ice skating in the park. It all seemed like a dream as she approached Southern California. The air was balmy; it kneaded palm tree fronds and hills that were dry, brown. Less than an hour later, Esther sat in her father's silver Lexus sliding through traffic. Her mother kept turning around and asking questions, smiling giddily and laughing. Her father glanced now and again at her in the rearview mirror and said nothing, although the creases at the corner of his eyes turned upwards with joy. The Lord is good, her father thought, his touch light on the wheel; the years turn to days and children leave and come back, each time for a shorter visit, and yet the Lord is good. A warm heaviness settled upon his heart; he felt he was no longer a young man; it was hard to speak.

Lifting his eyes to the mirror, Esther's father asked what she wanted to eat. "You want Mexican food, right?" her mother suggested, and she said of course; their first stop after coming home was always Mexican food. You couldn't find good Mexican food in Boston. Her mother laughed. Her father smiled. House-shackled hills and traffic lights sailed by in the night.

And yet there's a weariness beneath their smiles, unmoved by their words, as silent and still as an iceberg, thought Esther, leaning back into her seat; and she remembered her grandmother was dying. She closed her eyes. They exited the freeway, sped along wide, empty streets lined with palm trees and tae-kwon-do studios, jewelers and cleaners with neon lights; and when they got to the hill with the strawberry stand, the swinging of the car, the familiar motions of the road, the friendly nudge of the first, then the second, speed bump told her, without her having to open her eyes, that they were finally home.

A sharp fragment of dream.

Esther woke before dawn, strangely anxious and tense. The house was quiet and it seemed as if there was a light drizzling rain outside. Her childhood room had not changed. There was still the yellow duvet cover, grey in the dove-colored light, and the cherry wood desk and bookshelf her father had made. On the dresser was a lovely clutter of lacquered boxes, painted fans, books of fairytales, a bent and tarnished tiara with glass diamonds. Her bed was warm, soft, comforting. Again she thought of Isaac, that he wanted to propose to her, and that this may be the last year she'd come home for the holidays alone, and she could not sleep.

Out in the garden, she could now see what she could not the night before: the yellowing apple and pear trees, the stone lanterns glistening in the rain. Everything was dark, green, as if drowsy and glazed with the condensation of dreams. Downstairs, the Christmas tree abided serenely in the living room under tinsel garlands. The scent of pine freshened the air, made her think of snowy expanses; of a solemn, palatial quiet that could shelter a multitude of harassed and stinging souls, if only they could make it there.

Unlike her apartment in Boston, the house was warm. There were colored lights on the staircase railings, a vase of rosemary and a bar of peppermint soap in the bathroom. In the kitchen, her mother's apple cake rested on a white stand with scalloped edges. There was nothing lacking, everything more perfect than even her memory could have conjured. For the first time in her life, she thought how protected, safe and unblemished her childhood had been, how replete with luxury and satisfaction, and this new awareness troubled her. She felt afraid, weak, as if disaster loomed on the horizon.

She remembered her dream. Sometime in the night she'd awakened and seen a strange constellation in the sky. Two lines of stars were aligned as if in a funnel, the broad end positioned toward the horizon, and the distant sky was just beginning to pale when a silver light, the shape of a bullet, shot between the lines of stars. Up, up it flashed, as if aiming toward the moon, and then it fell upon the earth, her neighborhood, her house. Clouds of black smoke bloomed in the stunned air. The earth shook, held its breath before the *boom*. And then: action, confusion, a trembling, her dilemma over what to bring with her as they fled. She'd need her boots, she thought over and over, in case they made them march through the cold, the snow, the frozen air....

But it was only a dream. She lay on her back and gazed at the blue-painted ceiling and white fan. Gradually, the dim cloud light strengthened and adumbrated the different shades of grey in the sky. The sprinklers came on, chanting over the yard, *chuh, chuh, chuh*, and Jesus' words came floating over her like a chill: *for I have come to turn a man against his father, a daughter against her mother...whoever loses his life for my sake will save it...blessed are the poor and the weak and the persecuted.* She felt faint.

Once, in a fit of passion and joy, she had proclaimed to God that she would do anything for him, even if it meant sacrifice, death. She had been on a mission trip in Juarez, where the skeletal remains of cars sank into the dusty ground and she ate peanut butter and jelly sandwiches under a tin roof with children who had no shoes. The sky was blue, the air sweet with the scent of bougainvillea. The girls in her group squealed when they went to the bathroom (a shed, a door without a knob), because there was no toilet paper and they told each other they had to "air dry." Back at camp, they sang songs and sipped hot choco-late laced with cinnamon. *My Lord, My God: Holy! Holy! Holy!* beat her heart as they sang and the warm night seemed to encompass them with blessing. *I will follow, I will go*, said her heart in swollen exultation. It seemed so far from her now.

> Lying in bed, she recognized the praise and joy were easy, because she could leave Juarez, its rows of cement block shacks embedded in the dusty hills like desiccated honeycombs.

She had been so young, so naïve. Lying in bed, she recognized that the praise and joy were easy, because she could leave Juarez, its rows of cement block shacks embedded into the dusty hills like desiccated honeycombs. She could come home to granite counters, carpet, and hardwood floors. In the safety of suburbia, she could tell her friends there are wedding receptions at McDonalds. Imagine! McDonalds! she could say, incredulous, arrogant, utterly callous even as she preened and posed in her magnanimity. She had gone on a mission trip. She had done her duty, helped a neighbor in need.

And now Isaac wanted to become a missionary.

Esther rose from bed, paced her room, picked up photographs and stared at herself as a child, as a teenager graced with an insouciant, careless smile. Ignorant. Ignorant. She had lived in such ignorance. Looking at herself, she wanted to laugh; she wanted to cry and clench something between her teeth. They had been teenagers when they were sent into Juarez. All day they marched around in happy solidarity. They sidled up shyly to men feeding pigeons, fingered the colored tassels of scarves. In a café with a floor that was tiled and red, they ate pig rinds, sipped tamarind tea—sweet, viscous—and exclaimed how glorious it was to be alive. Thinking about it now made her shiver. She had read the news since then. Juarez: an abandoned city, picked over by drug cartels and a corrupt police. The "Murder Capital of the World" they called it. Death prowled the streets, purred in the engines of vehicles, in the corners, the closets, the dusty, deserted plazas with churches parched as bones.

Why? She had asked Isaac the night he told her in the snow. Why missions? Why North Korea? Why not France? Or Japan! He had laughed. (Why had he laughed?) In the snow, he had laughed and his breath came out in frozen puffs beneath the lamps on the Common. He kissed her nose. Because there's suffering, he had said. His voice grew serious. The situation there is terrible. Orphans wander. People make soup from strips of bark. He grew quiet. Because I cannot ignore the weeping of God. The tips of her toes in her boots felt like ice, cold, so cold, as if they would disappear. (The weeping of God! she thought. Why must you care about the weeping of God!) But the Lord is faithful, whispered Isaac, and there are ways to get in, to help those people in need. And (of course) it will be glorious, because they will see the broken healed, and joy upon joy, unspeakable joy! His eyes—she could see them shine. They glinted with something pointed and pure, lustrous flecks of holy flame. Joy! Joy! The word made her throat ache. Why do I love him? she thought as she pressed her face against his scarf, smelled the sweet-warm wool scent, secretly kissed the place over his heart as he talked and dreamed of sacrifice in the snow.

How much do I love him? Esther asked herself as she paced her room and the sprinklers chanted and the garden exuded the night and its mineral, mossy scent. She picked up a book, flipped pages, put it down, and ran a hand through her hair. As a child, sometimes she would wake early and see the light on in her father's study. He was a good man, a kind man, wired with the fastidiousness of a surgeon; and he sent her cards in Boston addressed to "Miss Esther Kono" written in a small, crabbed hand, extolling the joys of knowing God. But now, when she ventured into the hallway, the tiles cold against her bare feet, she did not see the light on in the study, and it was quiet, still.

Hours passed. In the other room her mother coughed. A flock of parrots screeched their complaints to a steel-grey sky. The intermittent roar of a lawnmower grated against the earth. Her father turned on the treadmill and she could hear his feet pounding. One mile, two, three, five, seven. He ran on and on, towards the wall of bookcases and a plasma TV. A gift, she thought to herself when she heard him pounding away, what a gift to have a treadmill in your own house, to run a marathon before you reach your plasma TV, and she put on her mother's rubber clogs and went out to sit beneath the lemon tree.

"In college, it had been colored underwear with lace and satin bows...Now it was something different: Bible verses on notecards, online sermons droning away on her...Marilyn wasn't sure which was worse."

What a strange girl, her mother, Marilyn, thought to herself as she rinsed dishes in the sink and watched Esther step gingerly on the grass, reach down to tap dew from the rosemary bush. This time she is not happy to see us. She does not want to be home, and this morning she remarked about how beautiful the snow is in Boston, thought Esther's mother as she dried her hands. The spinach spanikopitas were in the oven, and she still had to polish the silverware for the Christmas party, go to the grocery store, wrap presents. There were many things to do. But the family was together. (She realigned a Christmas tree in her collection on the bay window.) Christmas brought the family together, and because she was happy to have her daughter back home, Marilyn tried not to think of how much Esther changed each time she went away. A new dress, a new haircut, a craving for almond milk and caramel lattes, words like "pretentious" flowing from her lips; a hundred little tics and slips that no one but a mother would recognize and mourn because it had the scent and flavor of a mind, a touch, a heart that was foreign, unknown. In college, it had been colored underwear with lace and satin bows, and there was a certain brazenness about the hips and eyes. Now it was something different: Bible verses on note cards, online sermons droning away on her computer into the night. Marilyn wasn't sure which was worse. Outside, Esther stood at the edge of the lawn and squinted towards the sky, and Marilyn had the suspicion that she was praying. Her daughter had changed the most when she started dating the seminarian. She wore hoodies and basketball shorts and no makeup, and she was no longer interested in shopping and manicures (superficial, everything is superficial, she said.)

But she would not dwell on that now. No, it was Christmas and Marilyn would not allow herself to brood. She swiped soap across a plate. And when Esther's boyfriend—what was his name? Abraham, Isaiah—something Biblical, why did he have to be so blatantly Biblical? Isaac, that was it—when he came, she would be kind, warm, generous. Marilyn smiled to herself. She was not a hard-hearted woman. When she looked up again, she noticed Esther trudging across the grass wearing—wearing what? She squinted, frowned: something red on her feet, red shoes—Marilyn's red rubber garden clogs—"Esther!" She opened the window. "Are you wearing my shoes? I don't want you wearing my shoes! And—remember! We need bread from the store! And meat! Don't forget the meat!" She clutched at her dishtowel and closed the window. That girl is always using my things, Marilyn thought, shaking her head. What a strange girl, a silly girl, still such a child—a baby really—and to think that once they used to spend their afternoons playing with chalk, watching beetles pick out paths across the driveway, when now there was so much to do, still so much to do.

Around noon, visitors.

Cynthia, Mitch, and their daughter, Amy, arrived with a bottle of wine and a box of cupcakes. They had come south for the holidays, having driven down from San Francisco all through the morning, and the wine was from Mitch's vineyard up north, a rosé with a hint of raspberry and vanilla, echoes of white chocolate.

"Delightful!" said Marilyn, receiving the wine and their greetings with an inclination of her head, a smile. Delightful. The years—once

pale, opaque—had parted and uncurled like petals, and revealed that
her sister, Cynthia, had done quite well. Mitch, a successful designer
(the family had doubted him at first) and her daughter, now stepping
through the doorway with the grace of a dancer, wearing black boots,
black leggings, a little black purse with a golden zipper and a golden
clasp, were talented and intelligent. A beautiful family, thought Marilyn, hugging, patting, stroking arms, laughing, and Cynthia had gotten
fatter, soft, sultry as an opera singer with that voice, low and clear, that
poured into the room, with warmth, with spice, her lips curling upwards, purple and stained, as if by wine.

"You're thinner than a pencil!" said Cynthia to Marilyn.

"You must be tired from the drive," said Marilyn, wondering why her
family had not yet appeared. Where was Mark? Where was Esther? Her
husband and daughter were always so slow, so serious and quiet.

Mark appeared at the head of the stairs, descended upon the clamor
of enthusiastic greetings with a smile, a nod: serene.

"And Esther? Where's Esther?" said Cynthia, taking off her heels,
letting her toes uncurl, feeling the cold of the tiles filter up through
her black tights like a balm. Cynthia was tired of parties, of visiting
people, of family, of Christmas; her feet were tired, her thighs were
tired, her face felt as if it had melted and congealed several times since
the morning as she listened to Amy complain and Mitch play the same
John Legend CD on repeat for hours. And now she was here, at her
sister Marilyn's house, being shown the table, the lamp stand, the shelf
with dovetail joints that Mark made in his workshop, in his spare time,
between his duties at the hospital and the church. Everything was
very nice, she said, the work of a craftsman. He should consider selling,
making a website—like Mitch, who was into photography, had entered
competitions, had his photo of a squirrel cracking a nut featured in
National Geographic. Her voice rose, declared, swooped.

From the garden outside, Esther could see her mother and aunt
talking in the living room, and she knew that their smiles were pieces
of their armor, their shields in combat. They were comparing each other, no doubt, their families and their houses, minds clicking, whirring
with calculations faster and more precise than any gadget or app, and
soon they would go into the kitchen and commence the one shared
indulgence they looked forward to with equal relish all year: they would
saunter; they would sit; they would look at Christmas cards and gossip.
But not yet, not yet. Now they were engaged in combat. They leaned
and swayed and moved their fingers, made their rings glint behind

the glass of the window, gestured like characters in a silent film. Now Aunt Cynthia was talking, smiling, sighing. Now her mother was saying something, speaking—trying to speak—with conviction, but Esther could see that there was hesitation, doubt, a flicker of vulnerability, and she wondered if it was because of her. Because she was quiet and shy when she spoke. Because she was a writer—a grad student—without a publication to her name. Because she was in love with a seminarian.

Her mother bowed her head. Defeat? Armistice? Esther could not tell, but they were finished now, making their way toward the kitchen table where the box of Christmas cards already waited for them. Vain. Superficial. And yet she loved her mother, thought Esther, because she had tried, she had rallied her defenses against Aunt Cynthia, who could be domineering, ruthless, concerned only with success and the number of digits in a bank account. Unlike Aunt Cynthia, there were times when her mother had done it for love and not for conquest.

Esther did not want to go inside. She had many things to think about and her heart was heavy.

Do I love him? she thought, looking at the lemon tree. In North Korea (so she had read), there was no soap, no trash (no food), no water, and to be Christian was to be always frightened and then to be dead. She held a lemon, still green, in her hand, pressed her thumbnail into its flesh, felt the sting of juice on a shredded cuticle. Impossible! She thought. It was impossible, she mourned, and the bright sky, the radiant leaves, the warm patio stones encased her with an uncomfortable heat, a feeling of closeness that seemed like it wanted to crush her bones. It was hard to breathe.

Tomorrow was Christmas Eve, the day of the party. Tomorrow Isaac would come. He would meet her family for the second time. He would bring flowers and chocolate because he wanted to propose to her someday soon. He would come under Aunt Cynthia's scrutiny. He would be found wanting and poor, with no talent or potential because he wanted to go to Korea—North Korea!—as a missionary and had never been to Cancun and sucked on a martini from a coconut, or whatever they did there.

Her mother's red rubber clogs squelched on the wet grass. But God really was extravagant in his creation of the mornings, she thought, trying to inhale the cool, invigorating air. If she was still a child and the eucalyptus tree had not yet fallen down during a night of wind, there would be nothing better than to crouch in the sand by its roots; to smell the tang, the freshness of its leaves; to pick a piece of the hard, glossy sap trickling down its bark like liquid ruby, like droplets of blood, and add it to her collection in the silver necklace box with white satin lining.

But the tree was gone. She sighed. Her childhood: gone. Esther went inside.

Her mother and aunt bent their heads over photographs and cards. On the other side of the table, her father and uncle talked about Bitcoins and Teslas. Her cousin ate a cupcake, complained that she was getting fat; and the kitchen was bright, warm, and it seemed to Esther that she had not experienced such warmth for quite some time. Her apartment in Boston, the cold mornings, stained and sticky formica counters, endless meals of canned soup and rice, a life of pecuniary stress: it all seemed very far away.

Her mother brewed peppermint tea, placed more cupcakes on a plate. Around one, they were surprised by a brief shower of rain that rattled the glass table and the chairs on the patio.

"The Morioka's daughter just got engaged," said Aunt Cynthia. "And her ring is a two-carat."

In the living room, Amy began playing the piano—Chopin's Fantasie Impromptu. She leaned gracefully into the music with her lips puckered, reminding Esther of a duck. Her cousin Amy puckered her lips a lot, put pink gloss on them, batted her eyelashes at boys, and always she reminded Esther of a duck.

"Esther, when do we get to read your first novel?" Aunt Cynthia's voice enfolded her, shook her, like something dark, majestic—a wave in a tropical sea. Every year, her aunt asked, and her wine-colored lips curled up knowingly. She says it to humor me, to make conversation, thought Esther. She does not think I will succeed, not like Amy, who is studying to be a doctor, who has already performed as a concert pianist in an indigo dress covered in sequins. Her aunt was waiting, looking at her, smiling with that sly smile and glittering eyes. Esther nodded and frowned; she gazed into the distance to appear mysterious and wise, befitting a writer. "We'll see. Soon. Hopefully sometime—soon," she murmured, peeling a cupcake from its liner, and to show that it was inevitable, a cinch, without a doubt, she licked the frosting from her fingertips, and smiled.

The day of the party.
The hours materialized, began to swell, dropped off one by one in an endless trickle of activity. They washed the plates, set out silver-

ware, vacuumed pine needles from the carpet, arranged spiced nuts and candies in ceramic soufflé cups. Around lunch, the roast was put in the oven and its smell rose through the house. Sunlight came gliding through the windows; it ruffled on the tinsel and the wreaths, melted over the grand piano, its ebony wood, and as the afternoon gleamed and faded in the tips of the trees, Esther lit the rose-colored candles set in the bathroom by the sink, and on the tables, and near the fireplace made of stone.

Her mother disappeared into the bedroom, came back with damp, fragrant hair; a necklace of pearls; a black sweater dress and tights. A little past six the guests began to arrive—aunts, uncles, cousins, grandparents, bustling in with food, with coats, pulling off shoes. And then there was Isaac. He stood in the doorway. He was smiling and alone. Isaac. Her heart hopped lightly like a bird, on a branch, wondering if it should fly. She loved him. All day she had questioned, she had wondered; she had tabulated the price and peril of a future together, had felt her courage wax, then wane, through cycles of pep talks and prayer. But now it seemed all so simple: she loved him. "Isaac!" She blushed. She stroked his shirt. She buried her face in his clean scent. In his hands was a bouquet of roses and oranges—oranges hanging in a plastic bag—and she loved him. Her mother greeted him, gave him a hug, took the flowers, but Esther could tell that she was distracted. "Ah, you're here," her mother said. "It's so nice you're here." And she went into the kitchen without noticing the oranges.

But he was here. Finally. "My friend gave them to me," said Isaac, holding out the bag, almost as if he were perplexed that someone would do something so kind, so simple for him. And the party, it flowed around them, its voice at times loose and sparkling, at times strained, carried along in eddies of lilting music, the fluid notes of a piano, drifting from the stereo, from the snow and the pines of Windham Hill. The house was full, the rooms bright with lamps and Christmas lights. In the kitchen, her father opened the oven, and the warmth of the roast billowed and breathed through its spiced crust, dark, juicy, sizzling on the foil.

Esther took the bag. The oranges were hard, still tinted green, and she noticed that they were speckled with dirt.

"And you must be—the boyfriend!" said her aunt, small, round, her pasty face bright at the cheeks. She had already had a glass of wine. Her voice, it soared, swooped, rippled with a laugh. He is a handsome young man, but he is shy and unsure, and his shirt is wrinkled, Aunt Cynthia thought to herself. Poor Esther. But what can I do? When she's not my daughter? And again she laughed, because Esther was not her daughter, was not Amy, who was studying to become a doctor and had played piano in an indigo dress the night of her twenty-first birthday. (In the kitchen, Amy ate a piece of fudge, complained that she was getting fat.)

"And you are—studying to become a pastor?" Amy asked.

"A missionary," Isaac smiled, he was going to become a missionary.

"A mish-shon-ary?" said Amy, her voice dumping dollops of sound; she loved her voice, her face, her smile, knew that out of all them, she was the most attractive, talented, intelligent, and, quite simply, the best: "A mish-shon-ary?" she said again, laughed and puckered her lips.

What an imbecile, thought Esther, chewing on bit of cheese. Her cousin was an imbecile and the party was not going well. She felt the knowledge curdling in the pit of her stomach. Her mother was distracted, Isaac was uncomfortable, and if he asked her if she would marry him, she did not know if she could say yes, even if she loved him.

Now she and Isaac drifted on the periphery of the party. Already she felt as if there was a coolness surrounding her, a draft of incomprehension, a crevice, a crag, and that she had been untethered on a shaft of ice in a polar sea. (And is he Japanese? Her grandma blinked through her glasses. No, Grandma. He's Korean. Oh. His mother's not Japanese? No, Grandma. Oh. And his father...?) And if he were to ask her tonight? Or tomorrow...? Her mother would not approve. Esther and Isaac would not come home for Christmas if they were missionaries. They could not leave church at Christmas in Korea to come home—and what were Jesus' words? *Everyone who has left houses or father or mother or children or lands*...but she did not want to leave. She thought of granite ridges, unpainted splintering shacks, the mud and the dirt of the bruised and black road ahead of her, and she did not want to leave. Isaac placed his hand upon the small of her back, relieved her of her empty plate, deposited it in the trash. She remembered that when he was a child, his father had left him, and at his mother's apartment the past Thanksgiving, they'd eaten everything with kimchee. It was just the three of them—his mom, Isaac and Esther—and she had liked it better that way.

But now it was dinner. Her father was gesturing for quiet to say grace. They gathered together. They bowed their heads. In the dining room, off white ceramic dishes, they ate green beans and potatoes, fig tartlets, and chestnuts; they spooned soup, knifed meat, toasted with wine; they fiddled and twitched with their phones (if they were young) and talked about dying and disease (if they were old); and after the pie was cut and ice cream scooped, the red tablecloth littered with crumbs, her cousins declared that they were stuffed and bored and wanted to watch a movie on the plasma TV. A movie on the plasma TV! thought Esther: If only I could always watch movies on a plasma TV here at home on a warm Christmas Eve. She laughed, she wanted to cry: Yes! Let's watch a movie! On the plasma TV!

And Isaac was looking at her, had been looking at her all evening, first with tenderness, now with confusion as he tried to say her name and she ran away up the stairs. Her dress, soft, blue, slipped from his touch, like the memory of a dream. Had he done something wrong? He sat back in his seat. The windows were black. The candles had begun to sputter. Only the old people were left, sitting and drowsing at the table. In New Jersey, his mother would already be at the church, pedaling the organ. Their friends would be gathering, lifting their voices in song, in celebration, each holding a candle under a white paper ring that caught the hot wax. One day, he would be the one before the church, lifting his hands, saying a prayer—words that came naturally to him, welled straight from the heart. Unlike today. Today, he did not know what to say. (Do you speak Japanese? Esther's grandmother leaned over and asked. *Nihongo wakarimasu? Wakaranaidesune!* She giggled like a child.) He shook his head, smiled, said: "I'm sorry, could you repeat that...?"

He was tired. He had been on a plane all day, inhaling the same stale air for hours, eating peanuts from plastic bags, and as he approached the glittering California cities, he had remembered that in North Korea his grandfather lived in darkness. There was no light. From a plane in the air coasting over the land, except for the lone, ghostly, faint-hearted sequin of the capital of Pyongyang, there was only blackness and night.

And now Esther was angry, or sad, or disappointed—he couldn't tell which—and he had never seen her more beautiful. Here in a home filled with warmth, with light, the scent of pine and cinnamon sticks, she laughed, she swayed and floated like a cloud filled with moonlight, her hair dark and smelling of flowers, and he had never seen her so beautiful. It made him sad. (*Kankokujin kiraidesu!* said her grandma. He nodded and smiled.) It made him want to go into a dark room and fall into a deep sleep.

God, how I love her, he thought. Across the room, the piano gleamed and a line of photographs arrayed themselves in glass on the shelves. The bass boom of the speakers from the upstairs room rocked the floor like an explosion. Can I really take her away? He picked up a wine glass, felt the sticky residue of fingertips, rolled the last bead of red liquid in a circle at the bottom of the cup. The future, he knew, would not be safe, would not be like this house, this family, this life. It felt cold to him, filled with darkness and fear, and—he had to remind himself—and– and the glory of God! (It was so easy to forget.) He would not be alone, and she would not be alone. They would hold meaning and purpose in their hands, and see the broken healed, and taste joy, unspeakable joy!

But his soul was sad.

Lord, how can I do this when I love her, he thought. I love her.

And, smiling at her grandma, he nodded, picked up his plate, excused himself, and went to the bathroom where he closed the door, stood with the candles simmering in the dark.

The clocks trudged toward midnight.

Grandparents were bundled into sweaters and taken home, and now only a few guests remained. Aunt Cynthia drowsed on the couch in the living room, snoring slightly. Spilled sugar and coffee cups were scattered across the tables. Upstairs in a darkened room, the spindly light of movie credits crawled over dark, sleeping forms, and through the window, slightly ajar, came the twittering sound of something moving in the bushes. A bird, a possum, a rat: Esther could not say. She sat on the floor with her back against the couch, arms wrapped around legs, chin resting on her knees, listening to the sound of sleep-filled breathing; and when the credits finished and there was no more music, she got up and left. She could not sleep like the others; she had wanted to and tried but could not, and now she was tired.

She closed the door to her room. Through the door to the balcony she could see the dark outlines of eucalyptus trees and pines pressed against the sky, the sliver of a moon. She remembered that, as a child, sometimes when the moon was full, she would go out on the balcony and climb up on the roof, moving carefully over the asphalt shingles, lest the creaking wake her parents.

It was quiet outside. The balcony floor, blue in the moonlight, was overlaid by the yellow light from her room. Somewhere in the house, Isaac was wondering where she was. She sensed him moving amongst the furniture, running his hands along the edges of tabletops, praying slow and uncertain prayers. But she could not go to him now; she did not want him to see her when she was so sad, so afraid.

She climbed up on the roof. Above her, the sky shook out its trea-

sures over the earth, and she wondered how beauty could emanate
from the vast frozen expanse of the universe—the violence of it, the
desolation of it—to caress her cheek, the pale back of her hand, with
a touch lighter than air. Vaguely, she remembered her dream, the stars
aligned in a malicious conspiracy, but tonight there was no strange
constellation in the sky. All was still, full of peace, and she realized that
it was Christmas.

> "She climbed up on the roof. Above her, the sky shook out its treasures over the earth, and she wondered how beauty could emanate from the vast frozen expanse of the universe..."

Esther closed her eyes. Did Jesus, God of the universe, know eveas
a baby how he would die? Could a baby, even though he was the incar-
nate God, conceive of such things? She imagined Christ in the womb,
enveloped by the warmth of his mother; the sudden clenching and
squeezing; the cold shock of the world; a manger where there were no
flowers, no music, no celebratory wine. On a piece of blanket lay Mary
wilted from the pain, and there was hay in her hair; it stuck to her
sweat and her skin. No, thought Esther: perhaps Jesus did not know
or understand the future at that moment. But Mary did. His mother,
Mary, did, as all mothers do, through the pain of sudden emptiness.

The lights from the house fell in blocks on the grass. It was past
midnight. The guests were leaving. Down below she could hear the
faint sounds of voices, the engine of a car. There was a knock at her
door; her mother called out to her; the sound of footsteps receded
down the hallway. A bit of silky cloud stretched like gauze around the
moon.

And yet, is it possible? She wondered, looking at the full, effulgent sky, and she asked: God—is it possible?

In the morning, they would open presents in their pajamas. They would put Kenny G. on the stereo and eat slices of coffee cake with hot cocoa or tea. They would try on new clothes, swipe their fingers across immaculate touch screens, cut their hands trying to tear open plastic; and far away in that other part of the world, Esther would know, there are children with fists no bigger than walnuts, beggars sleeping in the snow, women so tired they can no longer weep: the broken waiting to be healed. Waiting for joy, unspeakable joy.

E.K. OTA is a Japanese American writer from Southern California. She has lived in Vermont, Kyoto, and Nagoya. She is currently living in Boston, where she is a student in the MFA program at Emerson College.

MARK BAUMER

Mark Baumer lives in Providence, Rhode Island, and works in a library. The three poems come from a manuscript title, "You Done?" His website is thebaumer.com.

Three Poems

The waiter / handed me a menu / and said / our special today / is / a broth / of / tiny / invisible / legless /
blind men / most of these / tiny men / are delusional
/ but / some are / conscious / and understand / they
are going to be / eaten / if you hear screaming / it
might be / the tiny invisible men / or / it might be
/ your imagination / if you are allergic / to seafood
/ you might suffer / one time / a lady came in here /
and said / I hope my forehead / doesn't swell / it immediately began swelling / after she said this / there
was nothing / we could do

This morning / I found a refrigerator / tipped over / on the sidewalk / and got worried / the sky was releasing / its stockpile / before I could / more worried / about anything else / I stepped / on / a twig / it woke up / the neighbors

And / sometimes / I'll ask a question / but / by the
time / I finish asking / it / I'm already / so bored / it
doesn't seem possible / to listen / to the response /
the other day / I asked this guy / if he was tired / and
I don't remember / what happened / to him / after / I
stopped /

The MANDRAKE

Jean Lorrain

Translated by Patricia Worth

When word got out that the queen had given birth to a frog, there was consternation in the court. The ladies of the palace would not speak of it, and in the upper vestibules there were only sorry expressions and tight lips that spoke volumes. The master surgeon who had carried out this fine delivery could not bring himself to bear the tidings to the king. He swiftly left through a gate in the servants' quarters, scurried off into the countryside and was not seen again. As for the queen, at sight of the monstrosity that had issued from her womb, she fell in a fainting fit.

When she came out of it, the king was at her bedside, his brow knit, and more frightening in his silence than in the fray at the head of his troops, crushing the turbaned miscreants from Egypt and Syria, all of them lecherous pillagers and pagans. His face was so terrible that the poor queen almost fainted again, but she regained control of her senses since her safety was at stake.

"This here is a fine achievement, madame," he said, looking deep into her soul. "It's the first time that frogs have been seen in my line. You must be under a spell, unless you slept a deep sleep beside some pond, in which case it would be a matter of questioning all the guards of the castle who watch over you, and a few others, too."

He tormented her now with a glare so cruel that the poor queen suddenly swooned and fell in her blood.

And seeing this, he slowly left the royal bedroom, believing he had said enough. Five years earlier, the queen had given him a beautiful little prince, comely like his father and mother, for Queen Godelive was one of the most marvellous creatures of the time, and the two of them made the most handsome couple of the reigning monarchies. And so this frog with her fat belly and skinny thighs, suddenly turning up in the family, cast a great coldness into King Luitprand's heart; and the queen must have considered herself fortunate indeed for having given birth five years earlier to an adorable heir apparent. This son, on whom the king doted, was actually as wicked as a one-eyed horse. He was the dread of nannies, whose hair he would make sticky with pitch when he was not slyly nailing the hems of their dresses to the floor. He liked nothing but action and mischief, and his greatest pleasure was to crucify live bats to the panelled doors or else to sit poor little bare-bottomed monkeys on the hot stoves of the kitchens.

This child was already promising to later become a great burner of heretics.

For the sake of this charming heir, the king would fain forgive the queen, but he ordered the immediate death of the dreadful little beast.

The queen recovered, only to learn of the horrible sentence. She listened to it dry-eyed and without too many regrets, for she was proud of her family's beauty and even more of her own, and her bruised vanity could not be consoled after giving birth to a monster. At about the time of the curfew bell she fell asleep quite peacefully, but in the middle of the night was woken by the faint sound of a baby crying in the next room and an old woman's voice humming a nurse's song. The queen felt a vague foreboding clutch at her heart. Though still weak, she found the strength to drag herself out of her bed in the high-ceilinged chamber, slip between her sleeping attendants, and push open the door.

In the middle of a brightly lit room, the oldest of the midwives present at the birth was sitting beside a cradle, while against the high walls some servant-women were crouched on the floor, dozing. In the cradle, in a white silk baby's bonnet adorned with pearl fleur-de-lys made for the royal heir, slept the frog, transfixed, her eyes wide open, enormous, the eyes of a sleepwalker. On her chest, her two little webbed feet held a branch of green box.

The old midwife was gently rocking the cradle with her foot and in a quavering voice was singing a very old air with these mysterious words:

> Forsaken by your family,
> You are dying of love,
> And your great bleeding eyes,
> When again will they laugh?
>
> Though to them you be ugly,
> My sweet beauty,
> With just a touch of kindness
> Adorable you would be.
>
> Your round eyes cry
> And fill them with horror,
> The heart is cold
> And life is a lure.
>
> Forsaken by your family,
> You are dying of love,
> And your great bleeding eyes,
> When again will they laugh?

And the frog's golden irises shone with tears!
She was dead, and the queen, who knew it, uttered a loud cry and fell to the ground.

Her ladies came running to revive her. The equivocal vision had disappeared; in the room beside her was neither cradle nor frog. The king's orders had been executed to the letter; the monster's head had been crushed between two stones and her limp corpse thrown into the castle moat.

The queen never recovered from the birth. From that day she lay in the half-light of her bedroom, beset by a strange languor.

There was henceforth a kind of invisible presence round her. She could no longer be alone; in her room there always had to be candles lit and waiting-women on guard; they relieved one another from hour to hour, terrified and silent, slowly bewitched by the queen's obsessive fright. And the whole castle was haunted with funereal shudders and an unspeakable creeping; a wild wind blew and something frightful prowled, born of Godelive's wild-eyed anguish. Sometimes, from her chair she would spring up erect with a great scream, then fall back down, perspiration on her temples, inert. In the night, she was visited by ambiguous nightmares.

There were times she dreamt she had been cast out by the king and was wandering slowly through the deserted streets of her town, alone, abandoned by all, walking hand in hand with the insidious frog who was already grown up and dressed like a little princess; for in every dream the frog was always there beside her and quite alive, and in her dreams her horror for the monster diminished each day; the large gold-circled eyes had such human pupils, and the frog's little foot, sticky and cool, clung to her hand so tenderly! Other times, she was transported through hot moonless nights onto sinister plains where pale grasses swayed at the foot of tall gibbets and a large black grey-hound followed her. She wandered, brooding, beneath the heavy beams of the gallows, the air thick with the stench of decaying corpses, and in the sulphurous night streaked with flashes from a storm, phosphorescent vertebrae were visible. The frog had disappeared, and the exiled, dethroned queen prowled like a she-wolf at the foot of the scaffold of justice, creeping up and unearthing the mandrake, the grisly root that grows amid mass graves, the obscene, hairy root whose fibrils affect the form of tense, skinny limbs spread out around a gnome's head, if with its bloated belly and vile cavernous genitals it can be called a gnome.

And she, Godelive, the queen repudiated from the throne of Thuringia and the daughter of the kings of Courland, she the very Catholic, very Christian queen, wandered at midnight in this solitary place, over these bleak plains, and with a keen eye she stopped anxiously at the foot of each scaffold where at times something tepid, like a waxen tear but strangely foul, fell onto her cheek. The tall pallid grasses, pallid as dead bones, rustled gently round her, so gently it was like distant voices or some obscure cry of a new-born child... And the feet of hanged men were silhouetted, ragged and black, beside her face; sometimes a large limp toe brushed her skin and the stench would be stronger. The flapping of wings greeted her in the darkness, from birds of prey woken in fright as she passed. Godelive continued to wander among the graves and their pestilence, feeble, faltering, but haunted by her fixation and reinvigorated with every passing moment by the dreadful hope she had in her heart. With her feverish hand, she sought the black greyhound walking in her shadow and was reassured as she stroked his sides. He stayed by her, disturbed and sniffing, drawn, like her, to the foot of the scaffolds by the horrible smell; and sometimes the queen heard a dull sound of mastication and knew that the dog had found what he was searching for. But she, who was still searching, pursued her deathly round beneath the fetid moisture dripping from the gallows, amid the grasses that whispered like a child crying.

The queen, through the oppressiveness of her dream, remembered very clearly the gruesome ritual that the Cabbala imposes on whoever wants to take possession of the magic root: tie a live dog to one of the fibres of the accursed plant, and while the garrotted animal is struggling, uprooting with every movement a little of the coveted herb, watch him covertly in the shadows, and when the mandrake is just out of the ground, throw yourself onto the panting beast and disembowel him with a knife. The life of the slaughtered animal then passes into the hideous root and animates it with the breath needed for swift, sure incantations.

The queen would wake, bathed in a cold sweat, knowing very well why a black greyhound was following her.

Now she began to surround herself with sorcerers and necromancers. An invincible attraction was driving her toward the occult sciences. It was as though she wanted deliverance from a spell and was anxious to break the suffocating circle of a curse. But, far from healing her, all these dark consultations aggravated her affliction. Her curiosity sharpened into something fevered and morbid, and nothing satisfied her anymore. The Evil One, now that she had half given herself to him, resisted her desire, and the frog still obsessed her.

Another nightmare also tormented her: she seemed to have been living in seclusion for some years in the middle of the woods, deep within a gloomy manor. The people and the king had forgotten her, and, in her solitude brightened by hawthorn flowers in April and snow in winter, she led a modest existence, almost happy, in the company of the frog who was attentive and affectionate as the gentlest daughter. She had become used to the frog's repulsive ugliness, and lived with her with not a word of protest, in a high room, rather dark and hung with old tapestries. The monster with an almost human face was always prettily crowned with field daisies, and over time her viscous little foot became unutterably sweet. The queen's shame for having given birth to such a monstrous creature lessened with the years and, on sunny days, she would go for a walk with the poor animal in the meadows and some-times take pleasure in it.

In the course of one of these sunny promenades, they went deep into a wood white with blossoming apple and almond trees; in a clear-ing the two of them came across a cortège of noble and peasant women in ceremonial clothes making their way to the chapel of a neighboring monastery. They were all happy mothers, or grandmothers of fortu-nate means, leading their progeny to the blessing of the Lord, for each woman was holding the hand of a pretty child with long hair crowned with roses; some even had three or four young brats hanging onto their skirts, girls or boys with a dawn complexion and laughing eyes.

At sight of these women the queen's heart ached, less from pain than from shame. Her whole being reddened at the pitiful garlanded frog hopping along behind her. She hastily drew the frog in close under the covering of her cloak, instinctively concealing her from their gaze. She was distressed by a sudden awareness of her immense misfortune; partly for shame, partly for terror, she held the mantle tightly closed round her. When the cortège had passed, the frog was no longer there, but a large blood stain soiled the lining: her incurable pride had killed her daughter a second time.

This nightmare made her life so much sadder that it was now mixed quite strangely with reality. She had left the court, and, virtually di-vorced by the king, who in the end was alarmed by the queen and her bestial pregnancy, a queen more preoccupied with magic than with the mass, she had to cede her position to a less dangerous, younger mis-tress, and, half condemned by the opinions of the people and the clergy, she lived henceforth in a small royal fiefdom on the frontier.

There she grew old alone, visited occasionally by her son, that handsome child who played cruel games and who was now a young man. He lived on bad terms with his father and cunningly schemed to come once or twice a year to spend twenty-four hours with the exiled queen, less out of filial respect than to aggravate the king's bad humor. These rare meetings between Prince Rotterick and Queen Godelive provoked old King Luitprand, driving him into a violent rage.

Now, the queen had got out of the habit of welcoming her son; his every visit had been followed by the departure of one of her waiting-women, for this Prince Rotterick was as debauched as he was ferocious. He loved evil for its own sake, delighting in the suffering of the body as in the pain of souls. He particularly loved to corrupt, and, served well by the great beauty inherited from his mother, he shamelessly attacked, sure of his conquest, all the sincere and chaste girls he would meet along his way; at court, it was the ladies of the palace; in town, the commoners' daughters; in the fields, the goose girls and washerwomen; in his mother's home it was the waiting-women.

A few noble girls had remained loyal to Queen Godelive in her plight, and now she saw them leave one by one. Because of this son, she was reduced to being served by woodcutters' daughters whom she scrubbed clean as best she could, though she had to hide them away and lock the gynaeceum when the watchmen reported the coming of Prince Rotterick. Once the hovering kite was gone, the poor queen would free her innocent doves and return to her needles and spinning wheel among her ladies, who were a little disappointed.

That was her life, between peasant women with little imagination and no conversation, dressed more or less artfully in the cast-offs from the royal household, and the sudden invasions of this son, who had become rare as fine days and destructive as hail, bringing with every visit a storm of threats and shouts to fill the vast muffled corridors of the chateau of oblivion. And the poor queen's loneliness was great.

In her early days of exile she had tried to amuse herself by indulging in some magical practices, but, deprived of the help of her ordinary astrologers who were well and truly hounded and banished by a royal edict, she had groped about in the dark and had as a result a personal experience which cured her of them forever.

One evening in June, a suspicious beggar woman came to the postern gate of the chateau and there, mysteriously, her eyes flaming beneath her hood, she left for the queen a coarse cloth sack, strangely sealed.

"If the object does not please her," the beggar added, "the queen will only have to have it put out tomorrow, after nightfall, on the third step of the Crucifix of Riffauges, at the intersection of the three roads. If on the contrary it pleases her, and she keeps it, she must put three hundred gold crowns in the same place, at the same time tomorrow; but in any case the object or the money must be in this same sealed bag; the treasure protects itself."

The queen kept the object: it was a sort of fibrous, hairy root, affecting the form of a monstrous toad or a still-born infant. With a shudder she recognised a mandrake, the mandrake that earlier dreams had revealed to her. A dead soul inhabited this root, she knew it from a trustworthy source, and she knew all the rituals prescribed for nurturing and developing this soul.

God, or rather hell, was thus giving back to her, perhaps, the real presence of the massacred frog. She devoted herself therefore to the cultivation of the mandrake. Enclosed in a bowl of dark glass, the human-shaped root floated, bathed in a nameless liquid. A death's head grinned close by, and a thin stream of sand ran continuously through a large sandglass, turned from hour to hour. After a week, the oil of the liquid had become a sort of reddish mud, the color of blood. At night the queen would get up to expose the bowl to the moon's rays, and in the daytime she carefully kept it away from sunlight, in a dark cabinet for which she always carried the key. Twice a week, strange beggars brought her grasses picked in the countryside, and day by day the head of the mandrake grew rounder, as eyes formed in its flat surface and little webbed hands twitched visibly at the end of its hideous fibres: the spell was working.

At night the queen left her bedroom door open to hear it sleep, for while the mandrake was inert during the day, at night it stirred and snored like a man. During one of these nights, the queen struggled under the most frightful nightmare. She dreamt that an improbable frog, enormous, almost human in size, was crouching on her chest and slowly suffocating her with its weight. She felt its icy webbed palms laid on her shoulders and the cold of its viscous belly sticking to hers. The nightmare lasted for hours; she did not wake until dawn, but waking proved it to be not a dream: the mandrake, all sticky with its oil, had furtively stolen away from its bowl and had curled up against her, holding her with its skinny arms, its hideous mouth suckling at her breast.

She was horrified, and with a cry she grabbed a foot of the strong-limbed root and wildly threw it out the window. It fell, in the full sun, into the mirrored waters of the moat. That very night a peasant child was found drowned there, his little hands caught in the hair of a root unknown in those parts.

From then on, the queen applied herself to prayer and never to magic. Her trials, however, were far from over.

One winter evening there were shouts and torches, murmurings and clangs of weapons at the door of the manor. It was Prince Rotterick. He asked for supper and beds for himself and his escort. But, this time, his audacity went beyond all limits. Behind him on his horse was a wench whose brocade dress shone strangely in the night; a wench, unless it was some young woman who had been kidnapped and ravished, a prey to his lust, for whom he was claiming a warm alcove and a rich repast. The queen, listening to her steward's announcement of the visit, had gone pale in her stall; outside, the horses were snorting and the riders were waiting impatiently. The queen, cold and still, could not decide whether to give the order to raise the portcullis.

"The girl is wounded and dying," said the steward. "She has blood everywhere, on her hands and on her dress. It's a coffin and a shroud the prince is asking for much more than sheets and a bed."

The queen stood bolt upright, hastily gave orders, descended the staircase of the donjon with great anguish of heart, and came into the lower room. Prince Rotterick was already there. His men, helmeted, masked and gloved in iron, were lined up along the wall. The prince bowed slightly before his mother and, showing her a heap of drapery thrown across the table, said:

"I found her crucified on a tree. She is in mortal danger. Please help her."

On the oaken table lay sprawled the most delightful creature, a young woman, white and tall, with a thick spreading mane of hair, black as ink. Her arms, her bosom and legs were bare. The brocade of her glaucous green dress glimmered and shone in the light of the torches. Immobile, her teeth clenched, she looked about her in horror; she held in her tightly-closed fists some strands of her hair with which she was trying to cover her breasts, but the palms of her two wretched hands were bleeding, cruelly punctured, and the flesh of her bare feet was also bleeding, painfully pierced.

All night the queen remained by the stranger's side. She washed and bound the wounds, settled the poor bruised body into her own bed, and the injured one, her eyes wide open, watched the queen without saying a word, without thanking her. All night, the crucified woman from the forest remained in a strange, disturbing position, her legs folded up, not so much lying as crouching inside the bed hangings. Her tragic face breathed not one complaint, not one sob, and the queen began to fear this silent girl whose gold-circled pupils were enormously dilated, improbably luminous in this barely lit room. Downstairs, the prince's incessant pacing filled the night with a rising sound of footsteps. From deep within the tapestry, frightening images loomed large before Godelive: they were the very characters of the high warp, young lords corseted in armor and ladies in hennins, but all of them deformed and reduced to batrachians, and the queen felt herself sinking into madness, spinning with vertigo. At about four o'clock in the morning, however, she fell asleep.

When she woke, it was broad daylight; the stained glass window was set ablaze with the rays of a rosy winter sun washing their amber light over the four-poster bed where the stranger was lying. But in the very place where a woman had suffered all night long lay an enormous frog, an almost human frog, and all the more monstrous. This frog was the young woman, for her four feet were delicately bound in linen, and under the animal's membranous eyelids the queen recognised the gold-circled pupils which two hours before had terrorised her, pupils which were now singularly tender. She recognized at last the frog from her dreams, the one which had haunted her, and which she had been missing all through the long nightmare of her life. In the same moment, the prince knocked on the door and asked to be let in.

The bloodied frog fixed two large pleading eyes on the queen; her whole frame was trembling with fright; and the queen, through the door, responded to the prince's demand, telling him to go and wait downstairs in the weapons room. Rotterick descended grumbling.

There, before all the prince's assembled men and all the castle servants, the queen recalled the whole history of her life, recounting the dreadful birth and the sorrowful nightmares during her churching and the nights of her exile, even including the recent sinister ordeal of the mandrake. All remained silent in horror, and Rotterick, foaming in his

lust, impatiently sneered. The queen, having made a sign for them all
to follow her, went back up to her bedroom, opened the door wide and
led the prince to the bedside.

When Rotterick entered he felt his hair stand on end; a heavy perspiration pearled on his temples. And Rotterick now understood, and
was afraid, for he too recognised the frog. He had pursued and hunted
it on his horse; and out of mockery and ferocity, once the animal was
caught, it was he himself who had crucified it to the birch trunk where
the martyred monster bled for a year.

And he could again see the monster in the rusty crimson of the Oc-
tober forest, the gestures of its limbs and its futile leaping, when he had
it surrounded by his dogs among the ferns and brambles. The beaters
had been alerted and this time were able to lure the animal far from the
ponds, and, chased down by the pack of hounds, the bleeding frog was
trying in vain to climb a tree trunk when Rotterick came hurtling out
into the clearing, leading his men.

His chestnut horse stopped in its tracks, and even the basset hounds
and Great Danes did not dare approach the frog; they bared their fangs
and sniffed, but were hesitant to bite: the fluid green animal repulsed
them.

Then Rotterick had his men seize the frog and stretch her, still pal-
pitating, upon the trunk of the birch, and while the whippers-in were
blowing their horns, he himself pinned the frog to the tree with four
arrows from his quiver, stuck into the bark, the blood, and the tears.

It was this bewitched animal that he was pursuing today in his
disgraceful desire, it was this swamp princess whom he lustfully coveted. He was of a cursed race like her, and, like her, was surely under a
horrible spell since they had both come from the same womb, issue of
the same blood. Then, glaring hatefully at the frog and his mother, he
drew his sword, and with a savage laugh hurled it across the lofty room
toward the bleeding monster. The queen screamed and rushed to the
bed. The sword crossed the room like a flash and flew into the high
stained glass window which shattered; but as it passed the queen, the
blade touched her shoulder, and Godelive collapsed at the foot of the
royal bed, her dress stained with blood.

All those present, distraught with horror, fled. The prince, alone for
a moment before these two heaving bodies, suddenly let out a great cry,
spun round, stumbled and hit his head against the wall, groped fearfully,

and finally found the door. He disappeared.

The chateau was now deserted; panic had emptied it. Under the postern arches, and under the porch vaults, left wide open to the air, the snow which had been falling since morning, silent and slow, began to heap up on the stone foliage of the colonnettes, on the relief figures of the pillar capitals. In the tall room, already dim in the twilight, the two bodies lay forsaken, but both were alive. Through the broken window, the snow penetrated the room, laying its downy velvet on the silk hangings glinting with shards of glass. And under the coolness of the snow the unconscious queen gradually revived. A small icy hand was fitfully squeezing hers, and in the darkened room where shadows were deepening, in her clenched fingers the queen felt the little cold hand slowly warming; the queen felt an exquisite tenderness flowing into her, but she kept her eyes closed and remained quietly slumped, both because of her wound, fearing she would arouse her pain, and because of this small hand and its human warmth.

This lasted for hours or for centuries, when little voices, strange, distant—no, muffled—drew her gently from her torpor; and these voices were saying: "Princess Ranaïde is going to die." And others responded: "Is Queen Godelive forgiven?" And the voices continued: "Blood washes away blood. Suffering absolves, sorrow purifies. Snow is a soft shroud." Then other voices, seeming to come from within the thick walls, were conferring strangely, speaking one after the other: "This is how the pride of a race is atoned for. Heaven hates the haughty. The heart of the great is hard. Pity flourishes in the humble. Too much arrogance produces monsters, but snow is a soft shroud." And as in a chorus, all the voices sang together: "Princess Ranaïde is going to die." In the darkness beneath her eyelids the slumbering queen saw her whole life again, and now she understood the meaning of her nightmares; it was the very life she would have lived and led with her daughter. If she had been able to protect her from death in her cradle, what crimes and tragedy she would have avoided! But a light vibration of wings brushed her head; wafting smells of incense transported her; the caress of a small hand warmed her own, and the queen hardly regretted the past.

All at once the sound of bells began to ring out in the night. A large snowflake came to rest on her face, and the queen opened her eyes, suddenly remembering it was Christmas Eve. She looked about her. The bedchamber was brilliantly lit; candles, candles everywhere, all of them held by wolves, foxes and even moles and weasels, all the wild animals of the forest curiously ranged round her. Here and there amongst their number stood a taller profile of a shepherd or woodcutter hooded against the cold. Animals and people were muttering prayers, and the queen was not surprised, knowing that animals talked on the night before Christmas. On the bed, the exquisite creature of the previous day, the white Princess Ranaïde, lay in the throes of death, a smile on her lips. The tapestry hanging on the wall now showed the nativity of Christ. Through the open door, other animals were still coming.

Queen Godelive felt two tears moistening her dry eyes. A small hand softly wiped them away. A child's voice whispered: "My mother!"

The next day, the two women were found dead. .

PATRICIA WORTH has a Master of Translation Studies from the Australian National University. Her translations have been published in Australia, New Caledonia and the US, including Jean Lorrain stories in The Brooklyn Rail and Eleven Eleven, and her translation of Spiridion, by George Sand, was published by SUNY Press in 2015.

JEAN LORRAIN (1855-1906) was a French author and judgmental spectator of fin-de-siècle decadence. He was renowned for his flamboyant homosexuality and an addiction to ether. Critics have often focused on his eccentricities at the expense of his works which portray his society and its obsessive fears.

The DEATH of Baldr

Samuel Martin

My son was five days old when someone first threatened to take him from me.

We were just home from the hospital, new parents with our firstborn, trying to get the hang of things—waiting for Liam's tar-like meconium stool to turn to seedy brown breast milk poop—when the home healthcare worker came by for a check-up and diagnosed Liam with jaundice. Not a big deal, I've since learned: three in five babies have jaundice. But my wife and I were not reassured that jaundice was a fairly common or easily-treated newborn condition. Instead, we were tossed a biliblanket—a stiff, plastic, blue-light tube—to Velcro-fasten around his belly and told that he *had* to wear it all the time for a set number of days. So, we gave it a test run, the home healthcare worker watching us closely, and Liam cried and Samantha found it frustrating to try to feed him tubed in that too-large, too-bright bionic contraption.

"Is there a smaller one?" Samantha asked.

"No," the home healthcare worker said, "he's just too small. You'll have to make do with this one."

So we asked if he had to wear it *all* the time, since it was so uncomfortable and affected his feeding. We were told sharply that they could track the number of hours the biliblanket ran and that if it did not run the prescribed number of hours then Child Services would take Liam away from us.

I feared losing my son before this incident. A vague memory of halting at the hospital's sliding doors, not wanting to take Liam out into the world. But having a state-certified health care professional threaten to take my son away certainly intensified that terror.

There's more than one way to lose a child, of course.

Miscarriages, for instance. Or feeding an infant water instead of breast milk or formula. SIDS. A too heavy blanket left in a crib. Abduction. An unfastened baby gate at the top of the stairs. Food or alcohol poisoning. Drugs. Drunk drivers. Pneumonia. A school shooting.

Those are the news-makers.

But you can also lose your child by not being present: being an alcoholic or addict, an absentee parent or a working one, depending on the job and its demands. My wife's fear is losing her boys to her job, working as the Assistant Director at an all-year camp for people with disabilities. For most of the year, except in the summer, she leaves the house before Liam is up, and returns an hour before his bedtime.

Samantha's struggle is finding ways to be present when her work keeps her away so much. So she plans her days off, arranging trips to the park or zoo, playdates, long walks around town. She sits down to play with Liam as soon as she walks through the door on dark winter nights, while I finish making supper. And she calls us on Skype when she works overnights on weekends.

There was a time when I thought the only way to be truly present in a kid's life was to be a stay-at-home parent. But even stay-at-home parents can miss things, as I've learned since being one: you can lose out, tune out, become numb for one reason or another.

It makes sense that we fear for our children, but this is not a modern phenomenon.

It's an ancient fear.

The first song in the *Poetic Edda*, a collection of old Norse myths said to have been written between the tenth and thirteenth centuries, is largely about this parental fear, or at least I infer this fear in the story.

I was reading a translation of the *Poetic Edda* the summer after Liam was born, when my wife and I moved from our home in Orange City, Iowa, to Sioux City, an hour away, so Samantha wouldn't have to make the long daily commute to work at her camp.

"I don't want to miss any more of him growing up," she told me the day we moved. She was buckling Liam, then nine months old, into his car seat and saying those serious words in a funny voice that made Liam giggle, his big eyes blue as the June sky.

Samantha cinched the straps tight and stared at our son, as if seeing him in some prophetic dream—older, detached, gone. I wondered if she saw the toddler in front of her or only her baby grown into a man moving out of our house, slipping away like daylight on her drive home from work in the winter.

I saw her begin to cry and turned away to throw another bag into the car.

It was the summer of 2014, and this temporary move was mainly for her sake, though there was a perk for me: we got put-up in a college apartment close to the camp. A quiet, slightly scuzzy, two room flat with a desk by a window, a full kitchen, and air conditioning. A contemporary hobbit-hole and perfect writing space, where I could work on my novel-in-progress. No household distractions like cleaning gutters, mowing the lawn, gardening, or tidying-up the garage.

No distractions, that is, except for Liam, who was then crawling around at a quicker clip and beginning to pull himself up on the furniture.

Many of my good friends are stay-at-home parents and full-time writers. Any frustrations or poop-on-the-manuscript stories I could tell would likely pale in comparison to the stories of these friends who somehow manage to run households and create original work and make it all seem par for the course. There was a time, writing my last book, before I became a father, when I romanticized these friends and writers like them.

Sure, I thought, they have all the time in the world to write, like when the kids are napping or playing quietly. Because what else do kids do but nap and play quietly?

I couldn't then decipher the wrinkles around their eyes, discern the difference between seraphed laugh lines and severe crows' feet etched by sleepless nights and a child's incomprehensible screaming.

Then I spent a summer in that Sioux City apartment trying to write a novel while being a full time stay-at-home dad.

I hazily recall finally getting Liam to go down for a nap, tip-toeing out of his room while trying to avoid the three squeaky spots in the floor, making coffee, settling into my chair at my desk in front of my laptop (internet clicked off, manuscript Word doc. open) and feeling absolutely exhausted—and not a self-satisfied, I just spent the afternoon working with my hands kind of tiredness. This was a particular kind of mind-numbing state I'd never experienced before wrestling a child to sleep several times a day. The kind of post-traumatic fatigue when all you can hear is the mental aftershock of your kid's crying.

All I wanted to do at those times was nap, but I knew that would be an hour of precious writing time wasted on beauty sleep. So I'd push through and try to get in-scene: try to make my characters move through the tired fog I myself was lost in.

Thank God for editing functions like cut and paste. Most of those sleep-deprived scenes have been either heavily reworked or scrapped altogether.

But I learned something on those days when I'd try to force characters through a room, try to imagine what they'd do or say or think: all while essentially intoxicated with lack of sleep. (Driving tired is the same as driving drunk, they say. I assume it's the same for writing). I learned that forcing myself to write while exhausted made me both a half-assed writer and parent. My scenes were clunky, the prose alcoholic, and I was no good to my boy when he woke up and wanted to play.

I also learned I didn't need to sacrifice one for the other—writing for parenting—like those egocentric who think their art is worth more than their families—who in many cases lose their kids, in different ways, in their pursuit of profundity and prose styles that will soon be all but forgotten. Not wanting to repeat their mistakes, I turned to certain women writers I know, who in their published essays and blogs taught me that I could strike a balance, but that to do so I had to listen to my body and my boy, which meant taking short naps right when I put Liam to bed.

Fifteen minutes or so: enough to reboot.

Then I could do household chores like laundry, dishes, and general clean-up (living in the apartment made these tasks minimal). And then, in the remaining time of Liam's nap, I could read over what I'd written the day before and block out scenes in a notebook, scrawl dialogue exchanges on shopping receipts I kept on my desk. Read a bit from the *Poetic Edda* or the first volume of Karl Ove Knausgaard's *My Struggle*—ancient and modern fathers' stories filling my mind as I tried to plot my story somewhere between those two extremes.

> "When I looked at Liam's sun-speckled face, I remember thinking how beautiful he was and wondering if the Norse god Odin ever looked at his son Baldr this way."

Then Liam would scream that he was awake and it was time for him.

All those notes I kept and the mental writing I did during the day (when I was alert and not dopey) guided my evening writing sprees after Liam went to bed and before Samantha got home late from summer camp. Between 7 p.m. and 10 p.m., five days a week, I hammered out the rest of that rough draft.

Once I found that rhythm—that balance—both writing and parenting became more invigorating. I was present: alert enough to remember significant moments with my son that summer, like that time I took him to Bacon Creek Park and lounged beneath a tall tree while I sipped homemade iced coffee from a thermos and he crawled off the picnic blanket and found pine cones and dandelions and other weeds, his face dappled in the late afternoon sun.

In moments like that I knew he'd hijack my novel in the best way possible. And he did that day, in a quick caffeinated epiphany that brought back the stories of portents and prophecies that I'd been reading in the *Poetic Edda*. When I looked at Liam's sun-speckled face, I remember thinking how beautiful he was and wondering if the Norse god Odin ever looked at his son Baldr this way. Not sure why I recalled the corpse-filled story of Ragnarök—the apocalypse of the northern gods—while staring at my son, except that I've always been intrigued by apocalyptic myths. Probably because I grew up a first wave Millenial (b. 1983) and was raised Pentecostal: a modern, evangelical form of Christianity that emphasizes end-of-days stories of the Rapture, the coming Judgment, and the Battle of Armageddon. My views on these things have changed over time, but I've never lost my fascination with—and terror of—those stories, which is probably why the myth of Ragnarök strikes me like a hammer blow to the brain every time I read it.

The Voluspo is full of ancient, biblical bloody-mindedness: its characters—the old gods—are obsessed with prophecy and knowing the grim details of the future. But what struck me that day—looking at my son's face and recalling that old tale—was how *modern* the story suddenly seemed. The Norse gods—in their naked desires and deep hatreds, their fearful bravery and broken love, their stupidity and scheming—could be Knausgaard and his family or people I know and try to bring to life on the page.

I've gone back since that day in the park and re-read the story several times. The poem is the song of Odin foreseeing Ragnarök and the death of his son Baldr. The dating of *The Voluspo* is contested by scholars, but Henry Adam Bellows has proposed a tenth century authorship by "a pagan Icelander with knowledge of Christianity." In other words: a writer living in a clash of tales—an age between ages, like our own, according philosopher Charles Taylor.

I imagine this writer trying to foresee, with the spread of a new religion like Christianity, what of the old Nordic world would be lost and what would persist. What, in the end, would rise from the churning waters of that chaotic time?

Myths like this shape us because they're both stories told and stories lived, simultaneously ancient and modern: tales of metamorphosis, shedding old skins for new. Stories of old fears that persist, even in our age of anti-anxiety meds. Anyone who becomes a father, in some way, lives such a myth. I know that as I was fumbling my way into fatherhood (which involved changing diapers, dreaming about changing diapers, and reading about Knausgaard changing diapers), I was struck, as I'm sure most parents are, by how my love for my son (despite and because of all that diaper changing) grew and bloomed in new and surprising ways. Like that sunny afternoon realizing just how beautiful Liam was: his dirty lips and serious face as he pulled up plants to taste them, spit dirt, and hold the roots up to the sun.

It's this strange, shape-shifting love I have for my son that has made me wonder about stories I know, ancient stories about fathers who loved their sons: Odin loving Baldr, whose death he witnesses but does not endure.

That day in the park, watching Liam play in the grass, pulling wild flowers and weeds and holding them up for me to see, I kept thinking of Baldr and the mistletoe and what mistletoe might be in the modern world.

The fuller version of the tale, found in the *Prose Edda*—written centuries after the *Poetic Edda*—says that Frigg, Baldr's mother, had demanded that all created things, save mistletoe, not harm her son. Being a god, creation obeyed her. But she left mistletoe out because it was a harmless plant, not a possible threat. Later, though, it became a sport to hurl things at Baldr, who could not be hurt by anything—that youthful immortality-complex you hope teens survive. Loki, though, another of Odin's sons, spitefully handed Baldr's blind half-brother Hoth a sprig of mistletoe, which Hoth hurled at his brother, killing him and bringing grief on all the gods, especially Odin.

The older version of the story, though, told in the *Poetic Edda*, is related as a vision told to Odin by an old seer: it's a prophecy of what *might* happen; a portent that must have scared Odin because he flew into a rage: the rage of a man terrified of losing his son.

It's in that fear—Odin's berserk terror—that I see his love for Baldr. (There remains, of course, the question of why Frigg's love for her son isn't mentioned. What does that look and feel like? Did she ever strap Baldr into a chariot and look at him like Samantha looked at Liam the day we moved to Sioux City?)

Writing the novel in that apartment, I thought a lot about that ancient story. But it was that day in the park, watching Liam pull up plants—any of which could have been poisonous, deadly as mistletoe— that I began to wonder: if my child was ever in danger, what extremes would I go to in order to keep him from harm?

What would I do if someone or something threatened to take him from me?

Back at the apartment in the days following, I saw Liam play in the room where I wrote: that college apartment that for all its strange smells and scuzziness was a kind of paradise. And outside it, the world—filled with poisons my son could ingest, like the Devil's Ivy on our bookcase back home; or the broken glass in the apartment's parking lot on which he could cut himself open. Those and a hundred other dangers: some invisible as a virus on an unwashed spoon.

I realized then, as all parents eventually do—as Knausgaard I think did in his six part memoir—that my son will have to live in this world of poison and betrayal. And what I want most is for him to know that I love him, and fear for him, and hope the best for him. Always. Knowing even now that I will see him wounded.

By others.

By me.

That's why that novel I'm still writing, dark as it is, has become a kind of love letter to my son.

I say "still writing" because that summer, as productive as it was, did not allow me enough time to finish the project. Life intruded. I had a very busy year teaching. Samantha got pregnant again—unexpectedly—and our second son Micah was born in July 2015. And, five days after Micah was born, I was informed that my tenure-track position at my college was being cut in the following year to save the school money.

Prior to both Micah's birth and my firing (which the administration preferred to call "right-sizing"), I'd blogged about a photo by Toronto artist Jonathan Castellino that I saw on Facebook—an image that gave me a way to think about my new writing practices since becoming a father; an image that, as it turns out, helped me stay with this novel even after being "right-sized" and being diagnosed, for the first time in my life, with depression.

It was the end of April 2015 when I saw the photo on Facebook. A Wednesday: my midweek get-crap-done day. And because it was the end of term that meant grading, tutorial meetings, and begrudgingly extending deadlines to students struggling to survive various apocalypses in which all their technology allegedly exploded (laptops, iPhones, and coffee makers) or all five of their grandmothers became seriously, seriously ill—"Like, maybe even dead." And, on top of my regular Wednesday to-do roster, I also had an eight-item addendum list that Samantha had me scrawl at breakfast on a newspaper page listing local yard sales to visit on my lunch hour, because Liam was nearing his second birthday and who in their right mind buys new stuff for toddlers when you can get next-to-new stuff at yard sales?

> "I watched a lot of pranks pulled from up in that choir loft. Hair snipped with scissors...a Roman soldier tripped by a shepherd's staff as he tried to outrun Mary, who was trying to get him to kiss the baby Jesus' bum."

So, like most people geared-up for a busy day, I poured myself a cup of coffee and did that modern form of mental yoga known as "checking Facebook"—*numbing*, my wife calls it—which is where I found that Castellino photo: "standards.wrought." When you look at the picture you're sitting in the balcony of an abandoned church—off center of the aisle and cross—staring at the sanctuary through a broken lamp strung from the ceiling like a divine lure.

Busy as I felt, thinking about my day before it actually got started, everything inside me stilled for one blessed moment when I saw that snapshot, like I was hooked and hauled back into the year-old memory of the Sioux City apartment, picturing Odin peering into that witch's well. It was like praying through a religious icon; as I stared at it, I felt as if I passed out of my own chaotic kitchen (I still hadn't put the dishes away from the night before), and slipped into that deserted sanctuary.

When I was a young Pentecostal kid in grade school, we performed our Christmas concerts in a church with just such a choir loft, and, oftentimes, I would sneak away from the busyness below—rehearsals, sword fights with mop handles and shepherd crooks, petty arguments over which of the wise men's turbans was the coolest—and I'd just watch the craziness, as if from a cliff top. Like I was Baldr hiding in rock-cut brambles, seeing Loki pluck a sprig of mistletoe below, and wondering what the trickster was up to this time.

I watched a lot of pranks pulled from up in that choir loft. Hair snipped with scissors snatched from the nursery. A Roman soldier tripped by a shepherd's staff as he tried to outrun Mary, who was trying to get him to kiss the baby Jesus' bum. I saw a lot up there, but rarely got in trouble because, as I pointed out to my mother—my second grade teacher and director of these school plays—I was in the choir loft, not running around.

I was above it all—not admitting I'd seen what I'd seen. I didn't try to alter events by lying and I never involved myself—just kept my mouth shut and played my part: the observer, the author—mute as an evangelical accepting God's inscrutable will.

God's will, I can accept.

But after I was told of my "right-sizing," I did not just want to accept the president's decision without somehow expressing to my colleagues my grief and, yes, anger. So I sent an email to staff and faculty saying I had wanted to tell them all the good news of my second son's birth: that our community had grown. But instead I had to tell them that though the community had grown in one way—Micah had arrived safe and sound—the community had shriveled in another way because my position had been cut in the "right-sizing" process.

Shortly after sending that email, I received a message from a woman who works at the college—a person I'd never met—telling me that my email had offended her because it seemed to question the administration's leadership of the college, a school she loves and supports. She felt in sending that email that I'd tried to hurt the administration and the school and, by association, her: using my son's birth as emotional leverage to get people on my side. She suggested that I "rise above" the situation and realize this sort of thing is just part of life, and in fact she and her husband had at different times lost jobs and been forced to move.

The message: Don't complain or question the administration—the board or president. Don't tell people you're hurt. And don't use your new son's birth as emotional blackmail. Suck it up. Rise above.

When people talk about rising above, I cringe because such talk, to me, smacks of holier-than-thou superiority: people who don't want to face things as they are—people who don't want you making *them* feel bad for not helping you.

My initial response to this woman was to tell her to fuck off.

In an email.

I remember trying to compose that message while Liam kept crawling over my laptop's keyboard. I'd shoo him away or give him a time-out and he'd cry and pout. It seems stupid now, but at the time I was convinced that what I was doing was important. Defending myself. Setting things straight. Cutting to the heart of the matter: *The college just needs a fiscal scapegoat and I'm untenured, outside the fold, and therefore easy to be picked off.*

Liam kept begging me to read to him while I wrote and re-wrote that email, whining for me to play trucks and tractors or go outside. And I kept telling him, "Daddy is working."

And what came of that work, all that shooing my son away and scolding him—ignoring him? I never sent the email. Instead of lashing out I sulked in long periods of numbed, brooding silence—self-pity a thick fog in which it became increasingly hard to hear the voices of my wife and sons calling out to me.

If I wasn't looking up and applying for other jobs, I was on Facebook, clicking refresh to get my dopamine fix—hoping I'd come across something: some good news or distraction—Liam crawling over my keyboard, begging to play, and me telling him repeatedly that daddy was "working" as I scrolled through links to other lives, career opportunities in Poland or posts about the consistency of my friends' kids' poop.

Anything to distract me from the life I'd lost control of.

In one of these online stints, searching for my next Facebook fix, I came across Castellino's choir loft again, and found myself wanting to slip into that photograph, those old childhood memories, and just watch this whole "right-sizing" process unfold: observe the drama without getting as caught up in it as I was—now embroiled in an appeal to the college's governing board.

I wasn't able to separate myself from my situation in a healthy way until my doctor diagnosed me in November with depression and put me on antidepressants, which did a great deal to clear the dark fog in my mind that'd been thickening since July.

Within two weeks of being on Zoloft I began to notice that Liam trying to get my attention no longer infuriated me. I still remember the first day he tried to close my laptop lid—a regular occurrence—and I *didn't* snap at him. Instead of brushing him off or telling him no, I let him click the laptop shut, and he looked at me with his huge sky blue eyes, a wary tilt to his head when I asked if he wanted to read a book, as if he was genuinely surprised and even a bit skeptical that I wanted to spend time with him—that I didn't have to "work."

Reflecting on this now, I realize that after being "right-sized" I did what I always do in tough situations. I hide in my shell. But because the problem didn't go away, like most of my problems do, I stayed hidden, lost in my Facebook fog. When things get difficult I retreat from life: I long for the holy monastic cell of my bed—a survival impulse that drives my wife wild. When I once pointed out that Jesus did the same thing when he fell asleep in the back of a boat after a stressful day of feeding five thousand people, Samantha pointedly informed me that I wasn't Christ, in case I hadn't noticed, and supper still needed to be made.

She keeps me grounded, and I love her for that. She reminded me more than once in the semester following my "right-sizing" that I needed to "get my head around this." There were still bills to pay, kids to look after, diapers to change, and dishes to wash. She never told me I couldn't feel hurt. Just that I couldn't shut down or run away or spend my whole day sleeping. Or on Facebook.

We now had two boys, after all. And she had to work.

I couldn't just stop being dad.

She told me to take more pictures of the boys, to journal or blog about the new things they did each day. Pay attention to them, she said, in much less direct ways.

Be present.

I know that being present takes practice, effort, contemplation. But I also know that depression can make such contemplation impossible. When I was at my most depressed, I remember holding Micah, my infant son—seeing him smile and reach for my fingers with his tiny hand—and feeling nothing. I couldn't father in that mental haze or break my Facebook addiction any more than I could write anything worth reading. When you're depressed—and I didn't believe this before experiencing it—you have no access to your mental choir loft, that room of your own—so like Castellino's photo in my mind—where you can think and write, where you're present enough to create.

When you're depressed, though, that door in your brain is chemically shut. The door is locked, but you know you need that space: that interior balcony—a clear, stilled mind.

You know you need peace.

And sometimes antidepressants are necessary to achieve such peace—peace that in the wake of depression seems to pass all understanding. In my case, tiny little blue Zoloft pills are the keys leading to that loft. That place where I am again learning to care for my children—that place from which I'm beginning to imagine myself back into my life as it is.

It's laughable, but I wonder if that's why Odin went to visit that old seer: because he was depressed. Maybe he'd heard talk of Christianity's growing influence in Scandinavia, rumors that his position as the *allfather* might eventually be "right-sized" to make room for a more popular Semitic deity. Or maybe he'd been watching Loki more closely and knew—in a way I assume only a god can know—that his son would betray him. Maybe that's why he went to the old hag: to peer through his mental fog and see things for how they really were. Find some way to face his reality, those last days of the gods.

Maybe visiting the witch was a way of forcing himself to be present for his son's sake, for his own sake—so he wouldn't have to lose Baldr twice, in prophetic vision and reality.

A deal with the devil, maybe, if there was a devil in those days.

As a Pentecostal, I was raised to believe in Satan's existence, but I wonder now what the devil looks like, what form he takes today, in my life. I've begun to ask recently: With whom—with what—have I made a deal in order to face my life as it is and not how I wish it was? Knausgaard made his deal with his publishers in writing the six volumes of *My Struggle*. He made a deal with the memoir form—the Norwegian-style, hyper-realistic tell-all—and that's cost him a few legal battles with family members.

Me? I take my pills. Pills that allow me to see—to really see—my sons.

But how to describe the effects of Zoloft?

I find myself in a frame of mind that in another age might have been a desert cave's mouth, where someone as emotionally disturbed as Saint Mary of Egypt could peer into the future and not be terrified: experience prophetic vision that allowed her to stick it out in the desert, to be a holy mother in the wilderness for the odd sick pilgrim who happened by.

She's the saint among all saints that I, a Protestant, venerate: the old seer I've adopted as a sort of spiritual mother, perhaps because of her charismatic, Pentecostal-like conversion. Legend has it that she set out on an anti-pilgrimage to Jerusalem, paying her way by offering sexual favors to other pilgrims. But in Jerusalem, when she tried to enter the Church of the Holy Sepulcher, she was prevented by an unseen force—a spiritual experience that prompted her to change her life and to pursue a calling as an ascetic in the desert, where she lived for the rest of her life. To me she's become an icon of what it might mean to give up a selfish lifestyle and to be present for others in the wilderness, whatever that wilderness might be.

When I was told I was being "right-sized," I looked into my future—my family's future, my boys'—and I was terrified, knowing just how arid the academic market is in my field. I feared my career would be sabotaged before it had really got started, and worried that without my income we'd be forced to move in with relatives, unable to pay rent.

Ultimately I feared being a failure.

And this fear numbed me to the greater fear of losing my boys, which is really my desire to be with them, to be part of their lives, a figure they'll remember. Not being remembered—or being remembered as an angry, self-centered asshole—is the Ragnarök I most dread.

Even so, I lost sight of that desire for my boys and became obsessed with my own failure and what that might mean for my family.

Then, unexpectedly, everything changed.

After a long appeal process, lasting the length of the 2015 Fall Term, my position was re-instated. What Tolkien might have called a eu-catastrophe—a sudden, joyous turn of events: Odin waking from his vision to find Baldr alive. Just like that my nightmare was over. A flick of the president's wrist—his signature on a letter saying he'd renew my contract in the coming year—and my upturned life was righted.

That good news came just before Christmas. It's after Christmas now—into February, close to Lent—and still I feel as if I've lost something. When I look around me, though, the world seems unchanged.

I feared losing my job and that fear has been forestalled—a fiscal apocalypse pushed back. I have a job and an agent interested in my novel; my wife tells me I'm laughing again; and my two boys seem unaware that I've been away a while: locked inside myself.

How did Julian of Norwich say it?

And all shall be well, and all manner of thing shall be well?

All *is* well.

But I feel as if I've given up on something. Or is it that I've given something up? I'm told Odin gouged out an eye to look in that witch's well, but I'm not missing an eye. I haven't technically lost anything. I haven't lost my job or my marriage or my sons, though I could have lost them all if I hadn't sought help—if I hadn't listened to Samantha and gone to the doctor's. I can foresee that much, if little else. I seem not to have lost anything, so why do I feel this way? Not depressed, but no longer whole either. I have lost something, I just don't know what that *something* is.

But I feel it lodge in my throat every morning when I take that little blue pill.

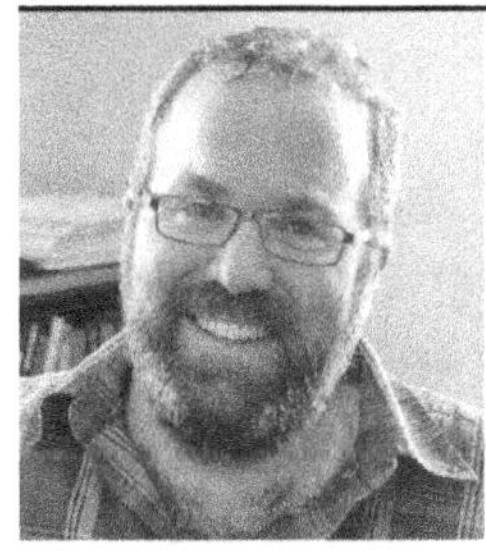

SAMUEL MARTIN is the author of the short story collection *This Ramshackle Tabernacle* (Breakwater 2010), short-listed for Canada's BMO Winterset Award, and the novel *A Blessed Snarl* (Breakwater 2012), nominated for the International IMPAC Dublin Literary Award. His short fiction, essays, artwork, and poetry have appeared in publication in Canada, the USA, and Australia. He lives in northwest Iowa with his wife and two sons, and he is currently at work on his second novel.

A.J. ODASSO

A.J. Odasso's poetry has appeared in a number of strange and wonderful publications, including *Sybil's Garage, Mythic Delirium, Jabberwocky, Cabinet des Fées, Midnight Echo, Not One of Us, Dreams & Nightmares, Goblin Fruit, Strange Horizons, Stone Telling, Farrago's Wainscot, Through the Gate, Liminality, inkscrawl,* and *Battersea Review*. Her début collection, *Lost Books* (Flipped Eye Publishing, 2010), was nominated for the 2010 London New Poetry Award and for the 2011 Forward Prize, and was also a finalist for the 2011 People's Book Prize. Her second collection with Flipped Eye, *The Dishonesty of Dreams*, was released in August of 2014. Her two chapbooks, *Devil's Road Down* and *Wanderlust*, are available from Maverick Duck Press. She holds degrees from Wellesley College and the University of York (UK), and she is currently a 2015-2016 MFA candidate in the Creative Writing (Poetry) Program at Boston University.

Outbound

Trackside again,
spellbound. I remember the drowned
girl, the haunted tower. Roving lakeside

here in the snow is how we courted. The stars
would brook neither of us, and you would not

harbor me. Dear heart of my undoing,
for you I'd have braved the spring.
Would've stayed.

Oblivious

It's your hair that tempts me first—
red ash and chestnut. What a catch

you must have been, I think, dizzied
by the speed at which you blink

behind lenses in well-thumbed frames.
The quirk of your mouth comes next,

that insatiable tilt in lieu of a smile
as you skirt my gaze. It's your hands

I get hung up on—thin digits, tensile
wrists. Your knuckles clamp book-spines

as you maunder, tautly halting my eye
at the half-round band on your finger.

The Calm Before

Evening primrose, bittersweet. This city's wish
is to stand long after we've left it. Drowsy green
will swallow our stories and crush them swiftly
to seeding. Ley-line and trestle-bridge alike
know our full stops, caesuras, palimpsests
before we've but breathed them. Our smoke
in the evening swan-wake shimmers patient
as frost. The next harsh winter stands waiting
already. Poison ivy reaches, tendriled warning
against restless belief. Yes, you will leave me
alone here in undisguised autumn. Your hands,
I trust less than this toxin-shine, your berry-rime
on my baited lips, so let me be. There's still time.

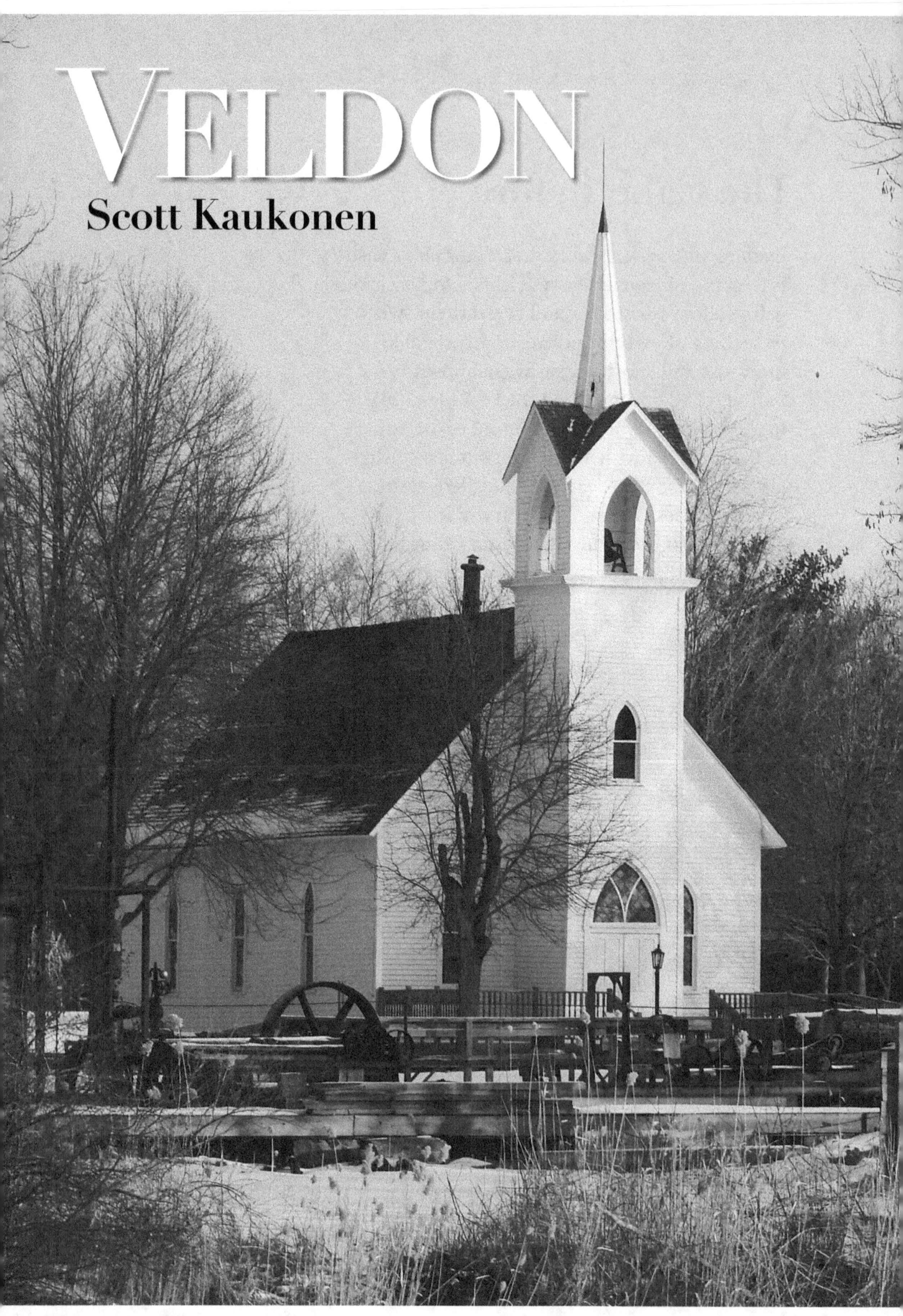

VELDON

Scott Kaukonen

The doctor told him he was going to die, it could be any hour now, or maybe not for a few days, but in any case, time was short, and if he had any business he wished to conduct before he died, he should do it now and not wait. When the doctor had left, Veldon called his wife upstairs to his bed, took her hand in his, and told her that he didn't believe in God and that he never had.

She didn't believe him. "Why, Veldon," she asked, "would you spend your entire life acting like you believe in God and doing everything you did, if you didn't really believe?"

He was seventy-two years old; the cancer was ravaging his body for a second time. There were moments when he thought he could feel it pulsing and sliding beneath his skin, its jaws ravenous, a black blob with teeth that ripped and tore. But it would be over now and soon.

"I knew it was the only way you'd marry me," he said. "If I told you I was a Christian. If I acted like I was a Christian."

She had been fifteen; he had been twenty-five. She had been thin and wiry even then; his own father had already been dead long enough for his son to have forgotten that that was why he had the farm. To say he was a Christian seemed a small concession to grant in return for the love of a woman. When he proposed, she said yes, and they married a few weeks later. They went together to church three times each week, did daily devotions together over the breakfast table and then with the children, prayed before leaving the house in the morning to work in the barns and the fields and at noon and evening meals and once more before bed; he tithed more than his share, became a deacon, went door-to-door on Saturday mornings evangelizing, taught Sunday school classes for thirty years, even on occasion sang in the choir; and always he'd been afraid that she'd discover the truth and leave him. No, not leave him. She did not believe in divorce. No, she would pursue him re-lentlessly; she would spend the rest of her life trying to get him saved. But he'd made up his mind about such things as God and man and the universe a long time ago. So he never told her. He never told anyone.

But before he died, he wanted to know if he'd done enough for her to still love him—even if he didn't believe in God and never had.

She said nothing, but instead went downstairs. He closed his eyes and waited to die.

Death didn't come that night. Or the following morning. He lay in his bed. He heard his wife downstairs. She moved about the kitchen preparing breakfast and then washing dishes. She loaded the dirty laundry into the clothes washer and then shifted the clothes to the dryer, then folded them on the kitchen table. She left the house. The car started and backed into the drive and then accelerated up over the lip of dirt and crusted snow and onto the highway. She was gone a long time. Then she came back. She marched straight up the stairs and into their bedroom.

"Where'd you go?" he asked.

"To see the pastor." She stood near the edge of the bed. Quilts were piled high atop him. He'd had trouble staying warm over the past few weeks. Plus, it was February. It was always cold in February anyway.

They had a young pastor now, a man in his late twenties, fresh from seminary. They'd had an even dozen pastors during their forty-seven years of marriage, a new one every two or three years. Most had been like this pastor, a freshly cracked seed, eyes brightened by the giant orb of the sun, ready to move along to bigger and better as soon as someone said they were ready, a piece of ripened fruit. On occasion, the church had inherited an old preacher, like a hand-me-down, a man wrung dry by life and the ministry, brittle as sheaves of corn in winter. Veldon didn't have anything against the new preacher. Some he'd liked rather well, especially those who knew a little bit about farming and raising hogs or hunting and firearms. The younger pastors these days, like this one, tended to stick to something like baseball or politics or even video games.

> ‘Don't sweet me,' she said. ‘God won't be sweet talked like that. That's what you need to think about.'

"What'd he say?" Veldon asked.

"The cancer must be addling his brain," she said, quoting the pastor. "You think so?"

"Ain't nothing ever addled you," she said. "He said it didn't seem possible to him that a man who didn't believe like you say you don't believe could've done what you done all these fifty years without it driving you insane."

"Forty-seven years," he said. "Maybe I just loved you that much."

"Don't sweet me," she said. "God won't be sweet talked like that. That's what you need to think about."

"Are you going to preach to me?" he asked. He'd listened to her preach to family and strangers for years now. She beat it into the children, and even after they were saved and baptized, she beat it into them some more. She wanted them to grow up to be preachers and missionaries, holier than holy. She didn't care about anything else. "How else could anything compare," she'd ask, "to the work of the Lord?"

"You think you need preaching, Veldon?"

He shook his head.

"You want dinner?"

He didn't want anything. He didn't have an appetite, not for food, not for drink, not for anything this world could offer. Nor the next world.

"I'll make anything you want," she said. "You want a steak?"

"No," he said. "I wouldn't be able to taste it anyway."

"I could get you ice cream," she said. She smiled wanly, and he managed to smile back.

"It's the middle of February," he said. "It's what, ten degrees outside? Cold as hell."

"Hell," she said, "ain't cold as anything."

He threw up blood that night. Heaved it up like a sick dog, and when their dogs had heaved up blood like that, he'd known what to do. He'd take them out behind the barn, out of eyesight of the kids, and he'd take his shotgun and he'd put a hole in the dog's head. Wasn't no way to get the kids out of earshot. They knew what it was to kill an animal; they'd helped with the pigs and the cows and all the rest, but the dogs were something different. At least, Veldon and Corrinne and the kids all acted as if it were that way. They acted, too, like it was something different when Grandpa and Grandma died, of old age mostly,

> ❝He wanted her to remember him as a young man, strong and vigorous, his big hands on her tiny waist, lifting her above his head.❞

heart failure and a stroke, respectively, or Luke from down the street who got his face caught in the auger, or Minnie, from church, who rolled her car six times before it blew up and burned her to death, or Clyde, who fell out of his fishing boat and drowned, or Nell, whose heart just up and quit at the age of twenty-eight. Veldon could go on and on. They'd go to the funeral home, show their respects. They'd say prayers for the dead and for those left behind. They'd make donations and send flowers. They'd act solemn while the dirt was piled atop the caskets. But he'd always known, deep down, that there wasn't a bit of difference. Humans just talked better was all.

When he was done heaving up the blood, he got down on his knees and cleaned it up himself. He didn't want Corrinne to see it. He wanted her to remember him as a young man, strong and vigorous, his big hands on her tiny waist, lifting her above his head. When she knocked on the door, he told her he was fine, he'd be out in a minute. He scrubbed with a rag of towel, which soaked through quickly, and then the toilet paper, which he piled in the stool. Every few minutes he had to flush the toilet, and still there was blood in the grout and on the rug until finally he gave up. He thought of the Blood of Christ and remembered the night he had been baptized, how stupid it felt, half-clothed, everyone in the pews staring up on stage as he repeated the words after the preacher, like an imbecile, some magical incantation, and then the preacher immersed him fully in water. He couldn't even remember which preacher it was, Jenkins maybe, the one who left for a church in Pennsylvania. Before Veldon and Corrinne married, Veldon had told Corrinne that he'd been saved as a boy at the knee of his late grandmother, but that he'd never been properly baptized at the time because they were Presbyterians and did not baptize by immersion. She made him promise to be baptized at the first opportunity, and the first opportunity came the week after the wedding. When they arrived home from the church that night, she made love to him in a manner that still shocked him all these years later, as if some plug had loosed and joy and desire overflowed her body, and it seemed more holy than anything he'd ever experienced, even the baptism itself. He could still remember everything about those minutes and how, while they were making love and for a period of time afterward, he thought maybe she had been right all along, there was a god, and his face could be seen if you just looked hard enough. But by morning, back in the fields behind the house, seated on the combine, the rows of corn stretched out before him, the feeling was gone, and he felt more like an animal that had needed to rut than a blessed and sanctified child of God.

That night she bathed him in bed. She brought a basin full of hot water. Fresh towels. She unbuttoned his nightshirt and opened it like a curtain. His chest appeared thinner and shallower than it ever had, the hair gray now, his nipples distended. She bathed him part by part, first dipping the cloth in the water and squeezing out the excess. She washed his face, laying the wet cloth across it and letting the heat of the water soak into his skin. Then she moved the cloth slowly but firmly across his chest and over his belly, which he had once been so proud of and which had become soft and slack in a matter of months. She washed his arms, paying careful attention to his hands, the nails that were long and yellowed now, and then she rubbed his shoulders firmly with the cloth until he started to cough again. She proceeded slowly, washing his legs and feet and his back, and even his most private parts, which had hardly been private to her, though it had been years since he'd looked upon her body with anything resembling lust. He could not speak for her. He looked away when she washed his penis, perhaps out of embarrassment, even he did not know. It seemed like a wasted part now, a vestigial remnant. But wouldn't it all be remnant soon enough? Still, she was sweet and tender with it.

He asked her if any of the children had called. She said they had not. He suggested maybe they could try calling them each tonight. They needed to know. He hoped they would all come home to see him soon. If he had one last wish, this was it. But he could not say that to Corrinne, who had other wishes, too. She had finished buttoning his pajama top. She was twisting the washcloth over the basin again to rid it of its water. He could see that something was bothering her. She would not look him in the eye.

"I'm not going to tell the children," she said. "I hope, for my sake, you will not."

"I won't tell them," he said.

She folded the washcloth in half and then in half again and carried it across the hallway to the bathroom where she set it in the sink. When she returned, she asked, "Why do you hate God so?"

"I don't hate God," he said. "I don't believe in God."

He thought about planting and nurturing and harvesting, long hard winters and baling hay, repairing the barn, paint and wire and two-penny nails, hard-bit frosts and the season they lost all the corn to a fire and the sickness that nearly swept away their entire herd of cattle one summer. He thought of the lean years and the few years of plenty, the milking and the slaughtering and the gelding and the shots, those long needles, and canning and births, his own children and the animals, for years it had seemed like there were always babies being born, coming out from between their mothers' legs, the afterbirth and the first cries, blood and mucus and shit. He was always knee-deep in it. They'd eat breakfast before dawn and read the day's scriptures, and they'd go around the table and pray. There were times when he planned to tell her: after the children were born and then after the children had all grown up and moved away, after both her parents had died, and then after Cleo blew his head clean off with the shotgun. Veldon knew Cleo had done what he done because the pastor then, one of the old pastors, had told him God hated him and what he did with his body. And Veldon didn't think much of what Cleo did with his body, how he used it with other men, and it was nothing Veldon would ever want to do with his body, but he thought that that was Cleo's business, not the preacher's, not God's, not anyone else's. Now he wondered if the pain and the cancer wasn't God's own punishment for his years of unbelief and deceit, a way to remind him of his own smallness in the world. But Veldon didn't need a god to remind him of his own smallness. Everywhere he looked there was nothing but smallness.

"'I don't hate God,' he said. 'I don't believe in God.'"

"If God heals you, will that make you believe?" she asked.

"God won't heal me," he said. "So don't bargain like that. You heard the doctor. I am not long for this world. What would you do if God didn't heal me then?"

"I have faith," she said. "He can heal you."

"Can and will are two different things," he said.

"You can't die now," she said. "I was okay with you dying when I thought you believed, when I thought I'd see you again in heaven. I knew it would only be a few short years anyway. But now you can't die. I don't want you to go to hell. I don't want to be apart from you."

He wanted to tell her that he wasn't going to hell, but he knew his wife's beliefs better than he knew his own. He'd always had a stronger grasp of theology than she did, though neither had finished high school and though he avoided writing whenever he could. She wrote letters every day, often to people in town she thought needed to be saved or needed to get their lives in order, or to their children who had all moved so far away, and though he could not correct her errors of grammar or social etiquette, he knew they were many, and this embarrassed him. It did not embarrass her who knew the Holy Spirit could

not be limited in its work by a few errors in punctuation or a few mis-
spelled words or offended sensibilities, the power of God being what
it was. He only read as well as he did because they had read through
the Bible together, the King James Version, most every year of their
marriage, dutifully performing their devotional duties every morning
and most evenings before bed. The latter had made things awkward
when they were young and he wanted to make love every night. She
always insisted first on reading the scriptures, the inerrant and divinely
inspired Word of God, so that after they had finished making love, she
could use the toilet and then go right to sleep. It never ceased to make
him self-conscious, more gentle and circumspect as a lover than he had
wanted to be.

He withdrew his hand from beneath the blankets. He wanted her to
place her hand in his own. He wanted to say, "We will not be apart."

But they always had been. All these years, and they always had been.

He did not die that night, and he did not die the following day or
the night after that. And then she came to him with an idea. There was
a new drug, not yet approved by the FDA and not yet available in the
United States. They'd have to go to Mexico. The pastor said they could
draw on the benevolent fund at the church to pay for the flight. Missionaries in Mexico City, the Oberlins—Did he remember the Oberlins? They'd been here four or five times; they'd even stayed here at the
farm on two occasions—would let them stay at their compound. The
Oberlins thanked the Lord for the opportunity to return the favor of
all those years of prayer, the monthly letters of support Corrinne had
written.

Veldon wasn't willing. He was in no condition to travel; neither of
them even had a passport; there were legal questions; they didn't have
the money to pay for the drug or the treatment, which would not be
covered by insurance; in fact, insurance might revoke its current cover-
age if they did something not approved; even Corrinne, when pressed,
admitted there was little evidence that the drug or the treatment
would work. She needed to accept that he was going to die; he had,
and it was okay. He only wanted now to die with dignity.

"Ain't no dignity in quitting," she said. "God has opened a window,"
she added, angrily. "You're just refusing to trust him and step out in
faith."

"I am stepping out," he said. "I just know there's nothing there to
catch me. There's not even anywhere to fall."

She didn't speak to him for three days.

Days passed, then weeks. It was a brutal winter. Every few days, it seemed, another Alberta Clipper swept down over the Upper Midwest and northern Michigan and dumped its snow and ice on the land; a permanent frost affixed itself to the windows of the bedroom, and Veldon had to press his palm to the icy window for several minutes just to create the smallest of holes out of which to look; everything outside seemed white—the barns and the road and the trees and the sky; the house seemed subject to an interminable cold, every draft and every leak exposed. The pastor came to visit, though Veldon had told Corrinne that he didn't want anyone coming to visit. Just the children. But they didn't come either. Always they gave Corrinne excuses.

Two months passed. He didn't die. But he didn't get better either.

Early one Sunday morning, with frost on the windows and the sun not yet arisen, Corrinne came to check on him. He was awake, seated upright in the bed against his pillows, a table lamp lit beside him. He wore his reading glasses. At first she thought he was reading the scriptures and it pleased her greatly, but then he asked her for a seven-letter word, Russian author, and she couldn't understand why he was wasting the last precious moments of his life on a crossword puzzle. Who cared about a seven-letter word for a Russian author? Who cared about Russian authors? She and Veldon had never gone to Russia and they never would!

"You feeling okay?" she asked.

"Okay is a good word. A four-letter word. Okay."

"Then okay enough to come to church with me this morning?"

He looked up. "Is it Sunday?" he asked.

She nodded.

He might have said no had he been able to think of a single reason to say no, so instead he said, "I might be." It seemed a small, last favor to her, even if it wasn't the favor she sought. So she went back downstairs to make him breakfast, eggs and sausages and pancakes, and he levered himself out of bed and washed up in the sink, the water cold and bracing. He found his best suit in the closet and a matching brown tie, dressed as best he could, and then made his way cautiously downstairs where he collapsed into his seat at the kitchen table. His fingers were swollen like a sow's belly, and so he had to ask her to knot his tie, though she didn't knot it too tightly and he left the top button unbuttoned so he could breathe. His insides ached too much to bend over to tie his shoes, so she did that for him, too. She brought his overcoat

from the entryway closet and his gloves and his hat, and after he'd
eaten, the most he'd eaten in weeks, and drank his black coffee, which
tasted good again, perhaps, he realized, for the last time, she set his
Bible on the table beside him and offered to drive. "Fair enough," he
said.

It was a four-mile drive into town to the church, a drive they'd made
thousands of times, and he nearly said that it was strange to know
that this might be the last such drive they ever made together, but he
thought the better of it. He would be dead soon enough and such real-
izations would be hers to make on her own. It didn't seem possible to
fathom that this would never happen again. Death itself seemed easier
to fathom.

The people in the congregation greeted Veldon as an old friend
reunited, the way the friends of Lazarus must have greeted him when
he emerged from the grave after that first death. Though a few noted
that he had lost a considerable amount of weight and that his skin
had turned yellow and tissuey, most pumped his hand vigorously and
slapped him on the shoulder, praising God and telling him that they
had been praying for him and for this day for weeks, and that they
had known that God would heal him, and here he was, God working
a miracle. The pastor even acknowledged Veldon's presence from the
pulpit, and people turned to look at Veldon, who smiled gamely and
gave a brief wave, a spectacle he'd never wanted to be. When they
stood and sang the hymns, Veldon stood, holding firmly to the pew in
front of him, and sang, as best he could, though the words were like
bits of broken concrete in his throat. When the pastor prayed, Veldon
closed his eyes and bowed his head, and listened, listened more intently than usual because he expected the pastor to pray for him, and he
wanted to hear what the pastor had to say. But the pastor did not pray
for him, did not ask the Lord to heal him or to ease his pain or to open
his heart to the truth of Jesus, and he did not pray for Corrinne, that
God might grant her strength and peace, now and in the days to come,
and he did not pray that the children of Veldon and Corrinne might
be comforted or that they might return home safely to see their dying
father one last time. Seated there in the pew that he had, over these
many years, come to think of as his own, Veldon stirred uncomfort-
ably. The pastor said, "Amen," and another hymn was sung, and a high
school student played, "The Old Rugged Cross," on a clarinet, and
then the pastor returned to the pulpit to deliver his sermon.

For the next forty-five minutes, Veldon listened as intently as he ever had to a sermon because he knew the preacher would be preaching to him, making one last bid to save his soul, and even if he never mentioned Veldon by name, the topic of the sermon might as well be, "Why Veldon Needs to Repent of His Lifetime of Sin and Deception and Find Jesus Christ as His Personal Lord and Savior Before It's Too Late, because It's Never Too Late until You Die and then It Is Too Late and You Are Burning in The Fiery Pit of Hell." But the pastor said nothing of the sort. He took his text from the second chapter of Acts and spoke of the early church and then of Pentecost and the Holy Spirit and how they owned all things in common, and when it was done, the pastor did not even give an altar call, just closed with prayer and another hymn (Veldon didn't even notice which one), then the benediction. It was one minute past the noon hour when the pastor said, "Amen," then the people streamed out, a few hugging Corrinne and telling Veldon that they would see him next week, "Lord willing." "Yes, Lord willing," he said without conviction. Then Veldon and Corrinne left, too.

When they arrived at the farmhouse, Veldon went to his room and undressed. He hung his suit coat in the closet and folded over his slacks and draped them on a hanger. He managed to loosen the tie enough to pull it over his head, and though he struggled with every single button on his shirt, he managed to unbutton them himself. Then he put on his pajamas and climbed into bed. He refused to come down for lunch, and by mid-afternoon, the pain had increased significantly, and he held himself still under the covers and told himself to remember the good times that had been his life. It seemed like the only thing he could do and a worthwhile thing to do while he still could.

He recalled the day he bagged his first deer, the low whistle of his father when an attractive woman drew near, the scent of his mother's bath lotion, a luxury she permitted herself on Friday nights after the children were in bed and her husband was in the living room watching the fights; he remembered junior varsity football practices, which he'd preferred to the games, which always seemed to take place in a blur, the games won or lost on the fringes of his consciousness, and he remembered, too, a particularly devastating block he'd laid on his childhood best friend one Tuesday afternoon near the end of that season, able still to recall the sound of that hit, his shoulder making contact with the center of the kid's chest, and the kid lifting off the ground and then landing, a long time later, it seemed, on the flat of his back,

the wind taken from his lungs; and he recalled briefly his wedding day
and night, though both had been rather unremarkable, they'd married
at the church and the reception had been held at the Grange Hall; he
tried to remember the birth of each of his children, though he more
easily recalled the afternoon he purchased the new combine, which
had carried them so far into debt. Then he found himself recalling a
particular day early in his relationship with Corrinne. They had not yet
married. She was probably fourteen; he would have been twenty-four.
It was shortly after the new year, and the town was holding an ice
skating party on the lake. They'd shoveled back the snow on a patch
of the lake behind the marina and put up a few advertising boards and
there was live music provided by the town's brass orchestra and hot
chocolate and skates for rent and fires where you could warm your
hands and your feet. It was a Saturday afternoon, and he'd finished his
chores on the farm that morning and had gone into town for supplies
and to drink a beer and go skating. He loved to skate, mostly because,
although he was and had always been generally a lug of a man, he was
a good skater and surprisingly graceful, everyone admitted. He en-
joyed their admiration. He didn't do anything fancy, he just skated fast
and smoothly, forward and backward, and he could stop and change
directions on a dime, and you couldn't help but notice him when you
saw him breezing effortlessly around the ice, his scarf and full head of
blond hair fluttering in the wind behind him, mostly because he was so
much bigger than everyone else, who were mostly children and young
women in colorful gloves and hats. He'd known Corrinne was going to
be there because she had told him she would be. Shortly before Christmas, they had crossed paths at the feed store where she was waiting
for her father to complete a purchase. Her father, Mr. Richardson, had
been close friends with Veldon's father before his untimely death, and
he'd often come over to the farmhouse in the late afternoon to talk
about farming or trucks, and little Corrinne would tag along, her own
mother home with yet another illness. He'd asked her that morning
in the feed store if she was going to be at the Christmas parade downtown later that day, and she'd blushed and said, "Yes," but first her
birthday was coming up and her father had promised her a new store-
bought dress, and so she was on her way to Ruth Ann's to pick one
out as soon as they were done here. Then she said he should come to
the ice skating party in two weeks. He hadn't made her any promises
because he wanted her to be surprised at his presence and his abilities,
though by the time the day arrived, he would have run over anyone

who tried to keep him from being there, even his mother, who could always find more work to be done on the farm. Within himself, he felt an irresistible desire, and it was for Corrinne, and it was sexual, and it was the most incredible feeling he'd ever had yet in his still young life. And she had been there, thin and tepid in her fourteen-year-old body, and he'd bought her hot chocolate and they'd skated together, slowly. She stumbled often. He blamed the uneven surface of the lake ice, the ruts from the other skate blades, the lack of courtesy of the children who darted between skaters, the witless parents who did not control their own broods. He did not try to hold her hand because she went to the Baptist church and she was not that kind of girl and besides she was wearing mittens and it would have been awkward and he wanted to touch her skin anyway, so they skated and they talked, their breaths forming small universes of clouds in front of them. She wore a long navy pea coat and a knitted blue cap and matching knitted mittens, and as the afternoon wore on, the early sun disappearing in the flat gray sky, she became chilled, her toes frozen stiff in the scuffed boots of her white skates, and so she invited him to come to the shore with her to sit beside one of the fires and drink hot chocolate. She wanted hers with marshmallows. He hesitated, shifting on his skate blades, and then he made what he thought at the time was the biggest mistake of his life. He said that he wanted to skate a little more. Then maybe he would join her. "Maybe," he had said. He hated himself for saying it the moment he said it. But it was true. He did want to skate more—not as he'd been skating with her, slowly and deliberately in small circles, each foot cautiously placed ahead of the next, slow glides, stuttered turns, her efforts labored, her apologies deflected aside as not a bother; instead, he wanted to skate hard and fast, his back bent, his arms pumping from side to side, his blood racing, like he'd seen once in a sports magazine. He wanted, above all, to be alone.

She said okay, and added that she'd had a nice time, as if she understood that this was the parting. He said he'd a fine time, too, and then she invited him to church on Sunday, "if you don't have anywhere else that you go." He said he'd try to make it, he hadn't been in a church since his dad had died, and there was always so much work to be done on the farm, but then he said he'd like to very much if she was going to be there. She blushed, and then they stood there awkwardly until she said her legs were sore and she needed to sit down before she collapsed right there on the ice. He helped her step onto the shore and watched her toddle her way to a bench where she seated herself and bent over and began to untie her laces. She didn't even look back at him.

A few minutes later, he had slipped beyond the official boundaries of the town's makeshift skate rink, and he was zipping along toward the center of the lake, his skates shushing beneath him. The sun had set and there was hunger in his belly and an early moon cast a blue glow over everything. In the distance, he could see the dark shadow of pine trees that lined the lake and the golden lights of houses along its shore. In his periphery, he caught glimpses of ice shanties, the names of the owners crudely painted on the wooden sides. If he had stopped, he would have heard behind him, far behind him now, the laughter of the townspeople where he had just been, people he had known since childhood, a few of whom he would know his entire life, and for whom this day, pleasant as it was, would soon dim to a vague memory. But Veldon was insistent that it would not be such a day for him.

He skated hard toward the middle of the lake, then turned toward his right and began to make a giant, swooping circle, leaning now toward his left, and then he did it again and again and again, trying to skate harder and faster each time he closed the circle, focusing on each stride, on each lift of his blade, on each full glide, his back bent, his muscles like pistons, his entire body leaning into the wind. He imagined that people near the shore were looking out across the dark ice of the lake and that they saw his silhouette moving over the frozen waters and that they admired his form and his grace, and that when someone said, "Who's that?" another said, "Veldon Dorn," and that they said it with admiration and that Corrinne heard what they said and thought, "Yes." It only made him skate faster. He swung his arms from side to side until the joints in his shoulders ached, and he breathed hard and deeply, his lips raw and blistered in the cold, wind-burn stinging his bare cheeks.

Finally, he eased himself to a stop, and stood there, bent over, in the middle of the lake, his gloved hands on his knees, winded. It felt good. Exhilarating. Like he could live forever. He was glad that he had not gone with Corrinne to the fire, that instead he had come out here on his own. Above him, stars appeared. Before him, the shore seemed distant and small, petty even. The fires flickered as anonymous bodies moved around them, and peals of laughter skidded across the open ice. Then suddenly he was overwhelmed by the need to get back to her and to ask her to marry him. He could not explain where the feeling had come from or why, how the spirit had moved him, if indeed it had, but he knew he must. Never had he been more certain of anything in his life and never would he be. Still, he resisted. He waited there, in the middle of the lake on his skate blades, the wind blowing through his sweater and pants, the skin beneath his clothes wet with perspiration, his toes numb inside his boots, his teeth percussioning violently, not wanting to leave that moment and its ache, because never had he wanted someone or something so badly, and he knew that the moment he started skating back to her, the ache would begin to fade and never would he get to experience that longing or that certainty again.

Downstairs, Corrinne put the dishes away. When she finished, she climbed again the stairs and stood silently at the bedroom door. She listened for the sound of her husband's breathing, but all she heard was a rushing wind.

SCOTT KAUKONEN is the author of the short-story collection *Ordination*, winner of the Ohio State University Prize in Short Fiction. His fiction has appeared in the *Chicago Tribune*, *Pleiades*, the *Cincinnati Review*, *Normal School*, *Barrelhouse*, *Third Coast*, and elsewhere. He's a past winner of the Nelson Algren Prize and an NEA fellowship. He directs the MFA program in creative writing at Sam Houston State University in Huntsville, Texas.

BIRDS
in the HEAD

Tonia L. Payne

The creek in the summer didn't have a lot to do with water. Even in spring, when the flow was greatest, there was still a lot more rock and gravel in the creek bed than there was anything liquid, although that hadn't always been the case. Willie's mom said that it used to be in spring the creek would fill all the way up—and sometimes overflow—with the runoff from the melting snows, but Willie didn't remember it ever being close to full. She said that it used to run so fast and full that it was a little dangerous to cross it; your feet could get swept out from under you and before you knew it you'd be floating along so fast you couldn't stand up again. It never happened to her, but she said a kid from the junior high had almost drowned one spring, goofing off in the creek when it was flooded.

Willie looked at the wide gray stripe of crumbled rock, moistened in the very center with the little wet brown ribbon of the creek proper, and tried to picture it filled with rushing, swirling water, but he couldn't do it. He crunched across the gravel, heading for the cottonwood on the far bank. Its creek-side roots had been exposed by one of those long-ago floods, and he liked to sit on them. They were a little bouncy and not really very comfortable, being too hard and too narrow, leaving a sore line across his fanny if he sat there too long without moving, but the shade was nice, and he could lean his back against the sharp curls and deep crevices of the tree's bark, ignoring the discomfort for the coolness and the sound of the leaves.

Mitch was a ways down stream, poking a stick into the water, squatting down close to look at whatever it was he could see there, or imagined he could see. There probably wasn't anything in the creek; it was too small for fish or even for much in the way of bugs. Maybe Mitch just saw a rock he liked—he was little enough to still be enchanted by just any old rock, not even the special ones. Tempe lay panting in the sun beside Mitch, staring up the creek and thinking dog thoughts. Tempe's real name was Tenspeed—Willie had named him that, thinking it was a fine, fast, lean-sounding name. Willie wanted to give him a name with a sense of the way he'd been when they first got him, all whippy and skinny and a little exciting, and thinking of the bicycle races he'd seen, picked Tenspeed as the closest he could get.

They had found him beside the road up in the mountains, up near the reservoir. They had been driving home from a day fishing, and saw this dog in one of the wide places where you were supposed to park your car to look at the view. Some people had been chasing him calling "Here, doggy, here, doggy," but he'd run away from them, trailing a chewed-off part of a leash. Something about him seemed very proud and strong, but it was obvious that he was also scared and maybe had been treated badly. Their mom said, "Oh no, oh, poor dog!" and pulled off the road. She had gotten out of the car very slowly, like she was about to step on something that she didn't want to break. The dog was close to their car, and the other people were waving to his mom and saying, "Look out, lady, he doesn't seem real friendly, he might bite!" but she didn't listen.

Willie had watched through the car window as she squatted down very slowly, holding out her hands so the dog could see they were empty. She just squatted there, and said in a very soft voice, "Hey, fella, hey, guy, it's okay, fella, no one's going to hurt you, hey, pup, hey, it's okay..." At first the dog had just looked at her, and dodged a little from side to side like he expected her to chase him or do something mean, but as she just stayed still, holding out her hands, he slowly came closer to her. He stopped once and growled a little, which made Willie very nervous, but his mom hadn't flinched; she just was still and kept talking in that quiet, comfortable voice, and finally the dog had whined a very sad, scared little whine and inched slowly over to her. He'd smelled her hands, and when at last he'd started to lick them, she'd very gently stroked his head, his neck. Willie felt a big ball of pride and excitement in his chest, like his mom had just done something almost magic. She stood up real slow, and with her hand on his neck, not touching the leash, had led the dog to their car—and that's how they got him.

But Mitch had been just a baby when they found the dog and was too little to pronounce his name right; it always came out sounding like Tem-pee. It had made Willie crazy, and he kept saying to Mitch "There's no such word, you dumb kid, it's Tenspeed." Finally, in frustration he'd turned to their mother and said, "Mom, there's no such word as Tem-pee, is there?" and was ashamed when she said, "Well, yes, actually, but it isn't English, maybe Spanish? I don't know what it means, but there's a city in Arizona called Tempe." Willie felt bad that he'd told Mitch he was stupid just because he couldn't pronounce Tenspeed, and because Tempe really was a word, so pretty soon, to make Mitch feel better he was calling the dog Tempe, too, and then their mom did, so now he was called Tempe all the time.

Willie watched Mitch for a while, trying to remember what it had been like to be four years old. He remembered things that had happened when he was four, but he couldn't remember being any different than he was now. He was pretty sure he'd done more interesting things than look at rocks in the creek for hours on end. Mitch didn't like to play the games that Willie thought were fun: Mitch didn't like to throw a softball around, or trying to break the bottles they found beside the road by throwing stones at them, but he could spend hours just looking at stuff. His endless examinations often irked Willie, as his slow, almost tender poking of the stick into the creek annoyed him now.

"Hey, Mitch," Willie yelled to him, and Tempe looked up and thumped his tail so the grit under it rattled a little. "Hey, Mitch, what the hell are you doing?" Willie felt a little guilty and shy to have yelled the word hell, and hoped Mitch hadn't really noticed. A lot of the kids at school were starting to swear; they thought it was tough, and so Willie was learning to swear, but it made him feel funny to do it, especially loud—like he'd stepped in something smelly on purpose. Mitch didn't answer but Willie could see him grinning. "Hey, Mitch!" Willie yelled even louder, with as much authority as he could muster.

"I can't hear you," Mitch yelled back, "I got *birds* in my head!" and he started laughing.

"What?" Willie shouted, his voice cracking a little.

"I can't hear you," Mitch yelled again, "I got birds in my head!" Mitch lay back on the gravel and laughed like he'd just heard the funniest joke in the world.

"Stupid kid," Willie said to himself, and then remembered. That morning when he'd been helping his mom get Mitch ready for their art class at the YMCA, Mitch had been in one of his more exasperating moods. Some days Mitch just didn't seem to be very interested in what was happening around him. He would barely eat and would have to be reminded almost with every bite that he was supposed to be having breakfast. When he was getting dressed, he'd sit on the edge of his mattress on the floor, one arm in his shirt sleeve, the other still bare, the shirt trailing off his shoulder like a cape while he just stared out the window high above his head. Willie was supposed to get them both ready while their mom was getting dressed, and they had to hurry so she wouldn't be late to her waitressing job, but nothing seemed to make Mitch pay attention. Finally Willie ended up dressing Mitch like he was still a baby, and as he did, Mitch suddenly said in a dreamy, soft voice, "Willie, I got a friend who's an elephant."

"No you don't, Mitch, you never even seen an elephant."

"But I do," Mitch said, still in that soft, tender voice. "I got a friend who's an elephant and he came to see me last night."

"You're nuts," Willie said, trying to get Mitch to step into his pants. Mitch kept sort-of falling over, and staring out the window.

"He did. He came to see me, and when I said I didn't have peanuts for him he cried and goed away," Mitch said, sounding truly sad about it. "He cried, and I said if he comed back tomorrow I'd have peanuts for him, but I don't know if he heered me. I think he did, though. He's a nice elephant. I call him Trudy, but it isn't his name."

"You can't call a boy elephant Trudy," Willie said, forgetting that this was an imaginary elephant anyway. "Trudy's a girl's name."

Mitch said with great dignity, "I said that's what I call him. I didn't say it's his name. Trudy is what I call him."

Willie was putting Mitch's feet into his sneakers, and pressing closed the Velcro straps they had in place of laces. *Baby shoes*, he thought, *I never had shoes with Velcro on them, I had ties.* Mitch was sitting very peacefully, looking at the sky out the window, all that was visible from their angle near the floor.

"You are a cuckoo head," said Willie, very firmly but quietly, right into Mitch's face. Mitch looked at him, startled, as if he'd just woken up. "You are a complete cuckoo head."

When they were in the car on their way to their art class, Mitch had said, "Mom, what's a cuckoo?" and, concentrating on the road, worrying about time, their mother said, "A kind of bird, honey." Willie waited for Mitch to say something about being called a cuckoo head, but he didn't; he just looked back out the window, thinking. And now, as Willie sat under the cottonwood, staring out at the bright sun dazzling on the pale gray rocks of the creek bed, he thought about Mitch saying, "I got birds in my head." *Weird what little kids come up with from stuff people say,* Willie thought from the vast age of eleven.

Willie looked at his watch, the Army one he got from his dad for Christmas. He was supposed to take care of Mitch from when their class ended at noon until four thirty, and then, since it was a day their Mom was working, not a day when she had classes, they would walk to the restaurant. It was a Mexican restaurant and was called Pepe's even though the lady who owned it and who did all the cooking was named Mrs. Viernes. Her first name was funny. It didn't sound familiar, but it looked like "cantaloupe" to Willie the first time he saw it spelled: Guadelupe. She was tiny, black haired, and very wrinkled, and at first both boys had been afraid of her; she seemed very mean. When their mom had taken the job at the start of the summer she had tried to arrange to work only until six, so she could get home in time to give them their dinner, but Mrs. Viernes didn't want to hire more than one waitress for each day and Pepe's was open from eleven until eight. The boys' mom told them later that she hadn't explained at first why she only wanted to work until six, but as soon as she did, Mrs. Viernes had said, "So, they can eat here." Their mom hadn't been sure about that, but Mrs. Viernes wouldn't have it any other way. "She says she's got plenty of food, what's a restaurant for but to feed people, and she insists it isn't an imposition. So we'll try it and see," their mom had explained.

When the boys went there the first night their mom was working, they went in the back door, like she had told them to, and Mrs. Viernes was there, chopping something green and spicy smelling on a big wooden block. She scowled at them, and shook her finger at them, and spoke a lot of Spanish very fast. Their mom came in then to place an order. She introduced them to Mrs. Viernes, and said for them to sit at the table in the kitchen and mind their manners, but then she had to go back out and take care of more customers. There was a young man with a long black ponytail washing dishes in a little room off to one side of the kitchen, but he never turned around, surrounded by the hiss and steam and clatter of his job. The boys sat at the table like their mom had said to. It was a small table with metal legs and a white top with gold speckles in it. It looked like something from someone's house, old and too little for a restaurant. Willie felt shy and kind-of stupid sitting there. Mitch looked like he was going to cry because everything was so strange. Mrs. Viernes had put her hands on her hips and stared at them for a minute, her lips pursed, making a little cluck-ing sound, and then she turned to the stove and started cooking. Willie was fascinated to watch her at the stove. She was so graceful when she was cooking and hardly looked to see where anything was—her hands just seemed to find things by themselves. There was something strong and proud about her that somehow reminded Willie of Tempe, although he felt a little funny comparing an old lady to a dog. But he couldn't shake the idea; they were somehow alike in their spirits.

Soon Mrs. Viernes was putting all kinds of things on plates for them and carrying huge amounts of food to where they sat. The chairs were the kind with metal frames and little padded plastic seats, and in the heat of the kitchen, Willie had felt his bare legs sticking to the plastic. He was afraid to move because he thought his skin might make one of those fart noises on the plastic, and he didn't want Mrs. Viernes to scold him for being rude, so he sat very still. Mitch still looked like he was going to cry. Mrs. Viernes pointed to things, and said their names in Spanish, some of them were names the boys recognized, but some weren't. There was one thing that looked very golden and a little crunchy and good (Chile Rellenos, Mrs. Viernes said) and Mitch took one. Willie helped him cut it up, and cheese ran out of the middle, so Mitch took a great big bite. He seemed to like it for a minute, and then his mouth scrunched up, and he choked a little, and finally he started to cry. Willie knew that part of why Mitch was crying was because he was afraid to cry in front of Mrs. Viernes, afraid she'd be mad at him, so Willie tried to calm him down, offering him water.

"Ah, no!" said Mrs. Viernes, but her voice wasn't sharp, and she wasn't talking to Mitch but to Willie. "Not water, it makes it worse." She took the water glass out of Willie's hand and instead brought Mitch some milk in a pink metal glass. "I'm sorry, kid, too hot for you?" she said as she handed it to him. "I forgot, you're not used to the chiles. Here, here, don't cry now, drink some milk, now just plain tortilla, will make it feel better," and she wiped Mitch's tears away, and suddenly hugged him tight for a quick second. Mitch stopped crying but seemed a little nervous about the rest of the food. Willie was a little nervous, too, but he tried a bite of the thing, the Chile Relleno, that had made Mitch cry and although it was pretty hot, he liked it, too, so he tried some other things while Mrs. Viernes sat down next to Mitch and said, "Okay, Mitch, let's see what you can try that won't burn your mouth so bad. Hey, this, it's just taco. You like taco? And this burrito, is not so hot..."

Willie forgot to sit still, and when he reached for a taco his leg made a real loud farting noise on the plastic seat, and he froze, embarrassed. He looked up at Mrs. Viernes and started to say, "I didn't do that, it was the seat," when he saw her pursed-up lips shake a little, and then she started laughing, just threw her head back and whooped with laughter. She looked at him, tears starting to show in the corners of her eyes and made a loud fart noise with her mouth. "BRRRRT," she went, and the boys were so surprised they started to laugh, too. Their mom came in with an order and said, "Well, I guess the ice has been broken," and for some reason that struck them all as incredibly funny, and they all laughed some more, even while Mrs. Viernes got up to go back to her cooking. From then on the boys liked having dinner with Mrs. Viernes. She wasn't always so nice; sometimes the restaurant was too busy for her to talk to them, and sometimes she just seemed mad, but they learned not to talk to her when she was like that. They knew she liked them and didn't feel afraid of her any more. Every time they left, after the restaurant had closed and their mom had finished setting up for the next day they'd say, "Thank you for dinner, Mrs. Viernes," and their mom would say, "Thanks, Lupe," and Mrs. Viernes would make a shooing gesture with her hands and say, "Ah, de nada, get out, go home." Some nights Willie looked back as they drove away, and she'd still be standing in the door of the restaurant kitchen, watching them go.

Willie sat thinking about Mrs. Viernes and his mom, and how the nights when Mom worked at the restaurant she seemed real tired but the nights when she had classes she seemed both tired and nervous. He didn't think words, so much as saw pictures, heard sounds, in his head. There was Mom at the kitchen table, wearing glasses, books and papers spread all around her and Tempe barking at kids running past the front yard while Mom shouted "Shut up, dammit!" her voice thin and tense. And then he saw Mrs. Viernes at the stove, and the guy with the long hair spraying water on the dirty dishes; then Mrs. Viernes in the restaurant's back door, the yellow light behind her, and his mother's voice saying softly, "Thanks, Lupe."

He listened to the quiet by the creek. Where he and Mitch were playing the creek was pretty far from the road, far from their house. His mom told him if anything happened he should go to their neighbor's house and ask one of the Miss Dabrowskis for help—one of them was always home in the afternoons—but their house was far from the creek, too, and sometimes he wondered if something bad happened to Mitch or to him when they were down there, where would the closest place be to go for help. He could make himself very nervous thinking about that. But mostly he didn't think about it. It was so peaceful at the creek, he only thought about stuff like that when he was sad or worried about something else. Mostly he thought other stuff, or just listened. Now, for instance, he could hear the high, tinny, wasplike noise of a motorcycle somewhere, and the gentle silky sound of the breeze in the cottonwood's leaves, and somewhere in the empty field behind him a couple of meadowlarks. A fly landed on his knee, sounding a lot like the motorcycle when it took off again. When it was real quiet like this, he almost could understand Mitch and his endless looking at things. As if his thought had touched his little brother, Mitch sat up and sang out, "Hey Willie! Willie, I can't heeeeeeear you! I got birds in my head!"

"I didn't say anything, you little nut!" Willie said, but not loud, and

Mitch sang so Willie could just barely hear him, "I can't heeeeeeear you, I got biiiiiiiiiiiiirds in my head!"

That night they were both in bed but Willie was still awake when the phone rang. He heard his mother's voice say softly, "Hello?" and knew she thought he was asleep already. He heard the crickets outside the window chirping in the quiet before she spoke again, and when she did, he wished he couldn't hear her at all.

"David, you've got to stop it," she said. It was the boys' father, and Willie knew he was probably calling from a bar somewhere, and that his mom hated it when his dad called at night like this. Their mother had never given any real reasons for why they got divorced, and Willie had never felt like he could ask their dad. She'd only said that she and their father couldn't get along together any more, and so they thought it was better not to try to live together and just get mad at each other all the time. But Willie knew, without knowing how, that his dad did stupid things, drinking sometimes, or spending time with the wrong people, with women; things that upset their mom a lot. Willie hated it when their dad called at night, because that seemed to upset their mom more than anything. He didn't know what Dad said, but he tried to guess from how Mom answered—and then tried not to hear it because he wasn't sure he wanted to know.

"I mean it, David," she said. Her voice was very calm, though she sounded sad, or tired, or both. "This doesn't do either of us any good at all....No, not this time....No....It's late, David, do you know what time it is?...Of course they're in bed....Actually, I was studying....No, nothing more to say....That's right....Goodbye, David."

Willie turned over, and saw that Mitch was awake, staring at the ceiling. Mitch looked at Willie for a second, and then looked away quickly. Willie heard his mom sigh, and then heard her pick up the phone again and dial a number.

"Mom?" she said, still in that calm, quiet voice, but then he heard her sort-of gasp and realized she was crying. "Oh, Mom, he keeps calling me...."

Mitch turned over fast, and his elbow thumped against the wall. Willie flinched, afraid their mom would know they were awake. She kept on talking, but her voice was harder to hear, so he knew she must have taken the phone into the living room. He relaxed a little, glad she still thought they were asleep. He looked at Mitch and saw that Mitch was crying silently.

"Hey, Mitchy," Willie whispered, and he lifted up his top sheet, "Come here and sleep in the big bed."

Mitch jumped up and climbed quickly into the bed next to Willie. It was always a treat for Mitch to sleep in a real bed, not just a mattress on the floor. Mitch climbed over Willie so he'd be next to the wall and wouldn't roll out of the bed in the night. Willie tucked the sheet around Mitch, and patted his head, not quite sure how to comfort his brother who was still shaking a little with the aftermath of tears.

"I hate it," whispered Mitch to the wall. "I hate it when she cries."

"Yeah," Willie said, helplessly, "me too."

"Daddy makes her cry?" Mitch whispered.

"Not always," Willie said, "but yeah, sometimes."

Both boys were silent for a minute, and then Mitch gulped and said, "Trudy won't visit me when Momma cries."

"Why not?" Willie said, curious about this turn of events in Mitch's imaginary world.

"He doesn't like it when she cries either," Mitch said, and started to cry again, harder. It was more than Willie could take; why did everyone have to hurt so much? He hurt too, but it hurt worse when he knew how sad Mitch was, and his mom.

"Hey, Mitchy?" Willie said, desperately, "Hey, kid, I know. Tell Trudy he can't hear Mom cry."

Silent, but thinking about this, Mitch slowly stopped crying. Finally, "Why can't he?"

"Tell Trudy he can't hear anything; he's got birds in his head."

Mitch snorted a little, something between tears and laughter, and Willie felt suddenly happy and strong, like he'd felt about his mom when Tempe licked her hand that first time, or like he felt about Mrs. Viernes's hands when she was cooking. He felt a tiny curling wave of relief, and a spreading pride.

"Yeah," Willie continued, riding the champagne bubble in his chest, "Trudy the elephant has birds in his head."

"Me too," said Mitch. "I got birds in my head. Trudy and me got birds in our heads. Hey, Willie, do you got birds in your head?"

"What?" said Willie, "I can't hear you, Mitch, I got birds in my head."

"Hey, Willie, what kind of birds are in your head?" asked Mitch, beginning to sound sleepy. Their mother's voice was now a quiet murmur from the other room. She had stopped crying and was talking about something else with Grandma, mostly listening. "Hunh, Willie, what kind of birds? Cuckoos?" Mitch said.

"No, not cuckoos," Willie said, and thought of the cottonwood tree, the silver creek bed, the tawny lark-filled field. "Meadowlarks."

"Yeah, me too," said Mitch. "Tee-dee, deedle-dee-deedle-dee-dum," he sang, barely audibly, trying to sound like a lark.

"Tee-dee, tweedle-bubble-dink," sang Willie, and put his arm around his brother, feeling the little boy's chest rise and fall as he slept, soft and easy as a breeze in cottonwood leaves.

TONIA L. PAYNE is a professor in the English department at Nassau Community College and assistant to the chair for evening supervision. Among her scholarly publications are "'We Are Dirt: We Are Earth': Ursula Le Guin and the Problem of Extra-Terrestrialism" (in *Nature in Literary and Cultural Studies: Transatlantic Conversations on Ecocriticism*) and "How Do We See Green? Ursula K. Le Guin's SF/Fantasy and the Environmental Paradigm Shift" (in *Falas da Terra no século XXI: What Do We See Green?*). She teaches fiction writing at NCC. Her poetry was published in *California Quarterly*.

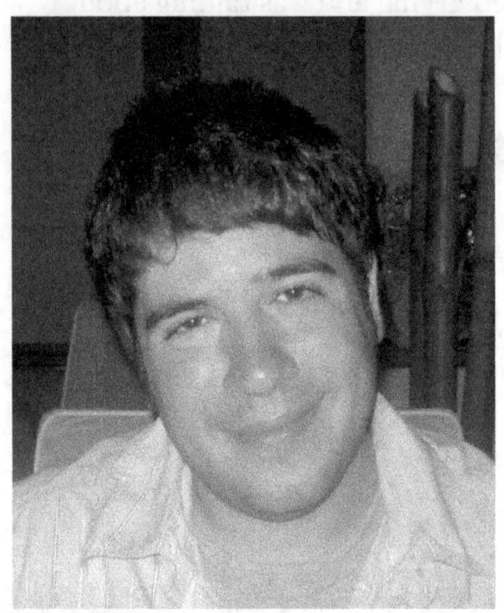

KEITH
MONTESANO

Keith Montesano is the author of the poetry collections *Ghost Lights* (Dream Horse Press, 2010), and *Scoring the Silent Film* (Dream Horse Press, 2013). He recently earned his PhD in English and creative writing from Binghamton University and currently works and lives in Pittsburgh with his wife and daughter.

First Light

Let us believe we own this world: the murmuration
of starlings with their cries and mimicry, bats weaving

through magic hour before the slow day we take for granted
winds down to dusk and its transient feel of leisure

and impermanence. Let us believe that our hands
will consume and then open—will graze and then release

from a forehead like ice or embers—our only conduit
to memory and desire, and let us believe that

when the seas dry up and the skyscrapers continue
to smolder, we will rise with our hands in each other's

to let the world, in that final moment, know that
if we had that choice again, nothing would change

but the endlessness of light as the only way to guide
our eyes to what we hope remains infinite and at last.

Slaughter of the Innocents

After the Painting by Marco Benefial, The Uffizi Gallery, Florence

I.

On the concrete seawall: rain and white star balloons
contrast black water, smiling stuffed elephants
and monkeys anchoring two thin strings, flowers

and a pinwheel just below them in the grass,
the only color in the frame near the clouds like fire
in the background, enveloping, as if to shroud

the water below it, entomb it for our lifetime.
Oh my God, I made a mistake, I made a mistake, she rasped
as the black minivan entered the water and sank

slowly enough for her oldest son to escape—
three babies buckled in the back, unaware of anything
but their inability to breathe. At ten, the boy was strong

enough to flee—before the windows wouldn't roll down—
and swim through forty-degree water to safety, unable
to see through the black surrounding his eyes.

I'm sorry. You have to forgive me, she said to a relative
an hour before, not waiting for an answer—
click of the talk button before disconnection

and dial tone, the mother of four gripping the phone,
not yet realizing she would soon say to her children:
If I'm going to die, you're dying with me.

II.

In the painting, the woman—whose baby's face
is nearly half off the canvas, looking directly
into our eyes—closes in on the man's groin with a knife,

poised to kill whatever it strikes. She holds
forcefully, arms wrapped so tightly around the torso
of her daughter that she almost strangles her,

as the man's left hand pulls down her clothes—chest
and stomach exposed—breaths and screamed pleas escaping
the woman's lips: a meaning we'll never know. All around:

newborns in the midst of dying, while another woman,
to the left, hands folded, either pounds her son's stomach
or prays with curled fingers. A bluish-gray, the child already

looks like a ghost, so it must be prayer: a prayer that she
will die with her son. The innocents thrash and fight
as well as they can, without weapons, wrapped

around their children, caught in this moment, a moment
the men in the distant background, on a balcony,
cannot see or simply ignore, while in a matter of minutes

blood will spill, black clouds will slide across the sky,
and the steps will be torn down years later: remains
in ruins, years of rain erasing wounds we'll never feel.

Into the Void

Celebrity Silhouette, February 2013

Just two weeks ago, on an Orioles cruise, Earl Weaver passed away
  in one of these rooms,
one higher than most, flush with every imaginable amenity:
  no surcharge at high-end
restaurants like Qsine and Murano, mini-bar always restocked,
  chamomile-cherry pillow mints,

free Wi-Fi anywhere on the ship. "Not a bad place to end it all,"
  someone says, and they may
be right, only a doctor friend of Jess's from her CME Conference
  follows: "If there's still
blood splattering the walls, did someone pay extra for his room?"
  The only forfeit

in Orioles history, ejections nearing one hundred, rule books
  torn to shreds and littered
over baselines: the legacy I knew nothing about until now.
  It really is something:
off the balcony, miles all around of just ocean-shimmer, shape-
  shifting every second,

with a horizon that's hard to mistake for a world that's truly round.
  And at night the crescendo
of a million turned-on faucets, where liminal becomes nothing
  but the darkness of places
even the mind can't touch. On formal night—surrounded
  by sagged skin, bad suits,

too much rouge and perfume—we wonder if the funeral has begun,
          and if we're all just silent
witnesses. Even in San Juan, docked for only hours, tourist traps
          sing with daiquiri mixing
machines and blood-red maraschino cherries, static-ridden salsa music
          and too-bright fluorescence.

In the fort by the wall at the edge of town, a woman at the highest point
          says to her husband,
"You wouldn't die if you jumped..." I check my pockets to see
          if she wants to bet on it,
but when I look up, she's vanished. Herded back on like bloated cattle
          by the tail-end boarding time,

I wonder how everyone truly wants this, while the waiters sweat
          to bring our twelve-top
braised short ribs and porcini risotto, all of us plastered with smiles.
          Afternoons, the grill
on Deck Fourteen never stops the fries, burgers, and dogs
          imminently making their way

through our bodies in slow descension toward the low levels
          of the world, finally
deposited in the immense ocean of our own grief, into what we all
          think we deserve.
So this is really what we're living for? To be the old divorced doctor
          popping generic Viagra

for the PA he's married to now, as he makes love to her in Hilton Head,
          and, when they're not there,
Savannah, as he jokes that the law he practices has nothing to do
          with medicine? Hoards
of dollar bills bar-coded into white tickets, paper-shredded into so many
          pockets that our knees buckle,

knuckles dragging toward oblivion like mini-earthquakes cracking every
        foundation in the suburbs,
in every gated home. We love the glittering lights because our eyes
        are going, the food
because Lipitor makes us never question each mouthful after mouthful,
        the servers because

their broken English makes us feel like kings. And when we're throwing up
        because of chemo treatments
or heartburn, we remember that though we don't deserve this, we'll never
        question why, as it's 8:30 now,
and our only concern is a long line at the Grand Cuvee Ballroom:
        the final walk toward the closing gates.

Listen to the SILENCE

Lisa Laughlin

*"And now there is merely silence, silence, silence, saying all
we did not know."*
– William Rose Benét

Evening had approached slowly after a sweltering day in July. As dusk crept upon us, there was an undeniable sense of merging—the sun was halfway melted into the dark silhouette of the mountains behind our house, and the shadows stretching across our yard blended tall blades of grass and pines into a dim hue. The layers of cool night air mingled with the heat of the day, and it was in a moment similar to this that my brother and I followed my father to the edge of the wheat field surrounding our home, walking through pools of warm and cool air on the way.

We often followed our father around when he got home from harvesting in the fields. From the moment we heard his Chevy truck rattle down the gravel driveway, we would sprint to the shop door and wait for him to step out wearing his leather work boots. Evenings were the only time we had with him at the height of the season, and after walking him to the door—while I carried his lunch pail and my brother his water jug—we would wait for him to take off his hat and grab a Corona and lime from the fridge and head outside.

Many nights like this we would lie under the stars and talk, watching the fields grow dark around us, but on this July evening my father was particularly silent. He was lying there, immobile, with his hands crossed over his chest, holding his beer and staring up at the sky. My brother and I stopped talking and waited for him to say something. I looked at the tall stalks of wheat next to us. The crisscrosses of the plaited heads so easily persuaded by the slightest of breezes in the daytime were utterly motionless, and the stillness made the night seem heavy.

"Listen, to the silence," my father finally said.

At the age of eleven, this perplexed me. I was determined to follow his instructions all the same, and tried very hard to listen for what he was hearing, but I didn't know how silence sounded. After a few minutes, I settled for simply staring at the stars that had reached their brilliant white. I didn't know what to listen for, but the stars seemed silent enough. I watched a satellite drift noiselessly across the fabric of the navy blue sky. I tried to think about what my father had meant.

Listen to the silence.

When I was in eighth grade, my school bus killed someone on the drive home one night. It was late November, and the narrow gravel road was consumed in a heavy fog. Our bus driver had been focused on the road, moving forward slowly and driving in the middle as one does in the country in winter. She knew how the steep ditches would appear flat, topped off with snow after the county finally got around to plowing. She knew the tiny pieces of gravel on the primitive road would be fused together with frost under the great black wheels of her bus, eliminating most of the traction. She heeded nature's caution signs; the other driver ignored them.

I remember the event in a series of still shots. Fog. Then headlights.

Then the sharp brake of the bus and flash of deep green and jolt of collision. Then silence. The front end of our bus had dipped into the bank on the right, coming to an abrupt stop. The crumpled green Jeep lay on its side in the ditch behind us across the road. Its headlights remained on, beaming at a skewed angle down the road before disappearing into the fog. Its interior remained dark. We seemed suspended in the seconds that followed, as if we were stuck in the scenes of a play—the only props in the world were the school bus and car with a backdrop of gray, and we were the actors who had forgotten our lines, frozen on stage, not sure how to act or react.

I remember the blank look in my bus driver's eyes that confirmed the moment. She had mechanically reached for the radio to call in the accident, but then she didn't know what to do with her hands. I remember her placing them over eyelids, running them over her salt-and-pepper hair. We stayed in the front of the bus together until the paramedics came: a half hour wait that seemed to span a lifetime. Aside from the occasional static crackle that escaped the lined face of the radio receiver, we waited in silence.

Afterwards, my neighbor had nightmares. She was a year older than me and talked about it the next day after school. She said she kept hearing the scream our bus driver made at the moment of collision. She recalled how low and scratchy the noise was, how unnatural it sounded. I couldn't remember the sound of the scream. I had only remembered the jolt of my shoulder against the seat, the silence that followed, and the stillness of the car already embalmed in the fog.

Later, on the night of the accident, I had watched a blonde woman on our television screen introduce the report with the phrase, *a fatal school bus accident.* The word *fatal* stuck sharply into the soft lining of my stomach, and I could feel the blood drain from my face. My mind told my body that it wasn't making any sense: that I'd already known the other driver was dead, that my stomach had already dropped the moment I saw the dark interior of that car and felt the silence.

What happens when silence marks the passing of a soul?

In February of 2007, my grandfather "Papa" died.

My parents had asked my brother and me to come into the living room and sit down, and told us that he finally passed. We had known about the lung cancer for a while now, and that it was only a matter of days before he would be gone (after all, my father said, he'd smoked almost continuously while out in the field, sometimes going through a pack a day while driving combine), but that didn't detract from the heaviness of the moment, or the space of time that followed when none of us knew what to say. It was in the silence that followed that I saw my father cry for the first time in my life. I was fifteen.

It took a moment to reconcile this man with the image I'd always had of him: my father, who never complained as he wrenched on machines in the field, his palms cracked and bleeding from the hard labor and psoriasis; my father, who delivered death, swift and unemotional, to our farm cats when they were irreversibly sick or injured. I remember sobbing over my favorite cat when I found him mewing on the ground, back legs paralyzed from feline Parvo. My father had calmly retrieved his shotgun from his bedroom and told me to go inside the house. I obeyed, but ran around to his bedroom window and stood on tiptoe to peer outside. I watched as he stood over the cat for a few seconds, and then shot it point-blank. I still remember the sound of compression traveling through glass. A moment later, my father had scooped up the body of the cat with a metal shovel, balancing its wobbling weight as he took measured steps towards the field and buried it in the dust.

On that afternoon when he told us Papa had died, he had turned away and left the room without another word. My mother had nervously tidied the table next to her and I went upstairs to my bedroom. None of us could stand to stay in the thick silence of the living room that seemed to suspend the truth, allowing it to linger and sink in.

I don't specifically remember my Papa's funeral, but I remember going to view his body.

We pulled up in the afternoon to the preservation home in our small town of Ephrata, Washington, and I remember thinking that the day was too sunny. It was cold, but too bright. My family shuffled through the door and came into a stale reception area, where small vases of fake flowers adorned most of the surfaces. They added to the strange stillness that seemed to fill the place. My parents signed a book and then ushered us towards the casket.

My aunt had already visited the funeral parlor and talked to us before we went. She said she'd been surprised with how good the body looked. I thought he looked like wax. He was the first person I had seen after death, and I remember the too-smooth texture of the rigid skin covering his cheekbones, the slightly yellow color of flesh that flooded his features, the absence of pores.

My family stood quietly in front of him. I remember trying to preserve the sight of him, lying there immobile with his hands crossed over his chest, embracing a folded American flag. I stared for a long time at the five-point stars, stark on the navy blue fabric. I can't recall what he was wearing, but I remember thinking about the green ink etched onto both of his forearms and biceps. One was a picture of a palm tree, another of a sailor. I've since forgotten the other two. They were tattoos he'd gotten when he was young and in the Navy, the once vivid lines now slightly blurred from the lifetime that followed. I had never really asked him anything about the war. His lips were pressed together now and I missed the sound of his voice.

After a few moments, my father turned from the casket and I followed him.

We often try to cover up the silence.

I have a faint memory of my mother teaching me how to pray. I remember her kneeling down beside my bed and me repeating her, solemnly, word after word. It's a clip in my memory: murmuring syllables as I stare at my mother's petite folded hands, my little brother a fidgeting shadow in the background on the bed across the room—but I know the prayer she taught me. I said it every night as the light went out for years after that:

Now I lay me down to sleep,
I pray thy Lord my soul to keep,
If I shall die before I wake,
I pray thy Lord my soul to take.

It became routine. Every night when my mother flipped off the light switch, I would squeeze my eyes shut and rattle off those lines in my head, clasping clammy hands in the folded way I'd seen her do. I was terrified of the dark. Not so much because of how it fused the shadows of my bedroom into otherworldly shapes, but because it gave me the suffocating feeling that what I could no longer see, was no longer there.

That nighttime made things cease to exist. At night my world was reduced to dimly-lit inanimate objects: the brass doorknob of my closet a few inches from my head, the darkened face of Ariel the Little Mermaid staring back at me from my bed sheets with an ivory smile. The outline of my brother across the room would have all but disappeared without the night-light I insisted on having.

These fears faded as I grew older and moved into a bedroom of my own, but the prayer stayed with me. So did a slight fear of the dark (I still had it firmly lodged in my mind that if I flipped off my own light switch, it was an inevitable fact that I wouldn't make it on the five-foot-sprint to my mattress.) I remember one particular evening when my father came up the stairs to turn off the light for me. He stopped near my closet door and plucked a glow-in-the-dark shooting star sticker from the furry tangle of my carpet. It had fallen from the ceiling where my scattered, make-believe constellations resided. He pressed the shooting star to the top corner of my closet door with his calloused thumb and turned out the light and left the room.

Suddenly isolated from the rest of the stickers, I stared at the shooting star for a few long minutes in the dark. Looking at it created a slight feeling of anxiety, but I couldn't place it, so I tried to brush off the feeling and closed my eyes. *Now I lay me down to sleep, I pray thy Lord my soul to keep, If I shall die before I wake*—and the rote flow of words stopped. I was suddenly baffled by the idea I had been repeating for years: what if I *did* die before tomorrow morning? Would I *know* I had died? I pictured both of my parents trying to wake me up unsuccessfully, tried to envision myself maybe floating above the ceiling like a ghost, like I'd seen somewhere. The thought wouldn't compute. I was perplexed by the idea of existing outside of my physical body, and fell into the mind-bending thought that followed: of simply *not* existing. Not thinking. Not breathing. Not moving. The silence would be staggering.

My eyes snapped open in the dark of my room and I stared at that shooting star, a small yellow-green silhouette. Then I looked out the triangle of my bedroom window at the real night sky. I was suddenly overwhelmed at the expanse of it all. I curled up in my bed and begged God to *just let me wake up in the morning, please.*

I could never figure out how to voice my thoughts, or sometimes just the overwhelming sense of isolation, to my parents. Instead, on nights when I'd get tangled up in thoughts of dying and far off stars and expansive universes, I would lie in my hot sheets, frozen, and stare at the single glow-in-the-dark star on my closet door.

If I shall die before I wake.

Sometimes the star was comforting in an odd way. Some nights it made me think of the day my own father would die. I imagined how, even after he was gone, I would still be able to lie in bed and look at that shooting star and remember him plucking it from its entanglement in the carpet, and I'd calm down.

Another night under the stars. It was early August, and my brother and I made our way to the edge of the wheat field barefoot, brushing over the dry grass as the heat of the day waned into a tangerine sunset. The earliest stars were arriving and we spread out a large, quilted blanket. Our father joined then, cracking open another Corona and emitting a heavy sigh. The air smelled of lime and salt mixed with the heavy scent of grease coming from his clothes. None of us felt the need to talk.

A breeze sifted over our bodies, and brought with it the first hint of night—a cool, earthy smell. I was staring thoughtlessly into the branches of a large pine tree wavering overhead when I heard my brother gasp. He pointed skyward and I spotted a shadow that had detached from the swaying mass of the pine.

"Nighthawk," my father whispered. I watched in awe as the bird plunged, twisting and zigzagging low above the heads of wheat. *Snatching up bugs*, my father explained. Another shape morphed out of the tree above us, then another, as four, five, six, nighthawks dove from their perches and became silent, low-sailing shadows.

I followed their erratic flight until the night deepened and their dark wings began to fade into the coal color of the sky. I could track one above my head at one moment, and the next I was staring at stars. I found that the best way to see the nighthawks was not to look for them at all, that it was easier to let my vision blur and follow the shimmers of black against black. Occasionally, I could catch a glimpse of the thin white band of their wings when they flashed by, but soon even that line lost contrast. They seemed to become part of the starry patchwork above, and we were left in the quiet darkness below.

We could no longer track their heavenly movements, but I knew they remained, and suddenly I didn't need the soft rush of their wings-to prove it.

The next time we talked about my Papa's funeral was five years later, on President's Day weekend in McCall, Idaho. We had become close with our neighbor family in the years following the bus accident; their daughter was my friend from school. Each year we traveled to snow-mobile in McCall for a three-day weekend, and that Saturday night the eight of us found ourselves packed into a single hotel room.

Our neighbors had just come from the funeral of their great-grand-mother, and it was the conversation starter of the night. The two youngest boys decided to detach themselves completely from the too-serious conversation, and went to watch a television show in the room across the hallway. I felt I was on the fringe of the discussion, but I didn't want to join the boys laughing at every punch line in the other room, either. I decided to stay a while and listen to the adult conversa-tion.

They began by joking that the lengthy, full Catholic mass of the funeral was nearly unbearable. They twirled the light, crystal stems of their wine glasses. Then they began to describe the casket.

I promptly left the room.

I drifted back and forth between the two hotel rooms: sitting on the bed next to the boys until I got bored of their constant fits of laughter, then walking back into the room of adults to see if they were still on the same topic. They were, and I was considering leaving again when my father started talking.

"Yeah," he started casually, "I viewed my dad when he died and I wish I never would have done it."

Questioning murmurs came from the other adults.

"It was one of the worst decisions I've ever made," my father said, slashing an imaginary line in front of him with his hand to convey final-ity. He went on to say that he could never get that image of his father out of his mind, that it ruined how he remembered him in life. My mother chimed in about how my Papa looked worse in his coffin than he did on his deathbed. I left the room again.

I decided in that moment, in that hotel hallway, that I would never view my father's body after he died if I were given the chance. I was stunned to discover it haunted him so: my father who didn't cry, my father who wasn't afraid of the dark, my father who could calmly view death glancing along the barrel of a shotgun. I was beginning to understand that those quiet moments could be loud.

I wonder what my father hears in the silence.

When my father dies, I hope it is a cloudless evening. I hope I'll be able to sit under the night sky, embalmed in the shadows, as we had. I want to see shimmers of black and know, for certain, that there are still nighthawks out there, making their heavenly rounds. Maybe then I'll hear what my father heard in the silence, and understand it. That way, later, when I have children, I can tell them to listen: I'll pluck up their shooting stars that have fallen to the carpet; I'll teach them to pray; I'll tell them about the nighthawks.

LISA LAUGHLIN is an Eastern Washington native who grew up on a dryland wheat farm. She received a B.A. in creative writing from the University of Idaho and is pursuing an MFA at Eastern Washington University in the creative nonfiction program. She has contributed to Orion's Place Where You Live Section and Hippocampus magazine, and she enjoys creating a sense of place in her writing to examine human connection with the land.

Fame by Another Name:

The Art of Ghostwriting

"What makes a story believable is if you can disappear into it." Writer Kevin Kaiser lives by this mantra, which may not seem an unusual approach to anyone who has ever been consumed by a creative pursuit, until you realize he intends to do just that—*disappear*, with the only traces of his identity blended indistinguishably to the story. His job is to be a ghost, and with that, to ensure that few are aware of his existence.

To ghostwrite is to truly test your storytelling talent—and perhaps your very passion for writing. Ghostwriters must be skilled manipulators of language and narrative, able to create a work void of their own voice. They must embody another person in their writing, from the distinct arc of the story down to the intricacies of writing patterns, syntax, diction. The objective is to vanish into the story and ultimately behind another person's identity. So why would a writer with such obvious talent—that which extends beyond the yawping of one's *own* story—be satisfied with writing in the shadows? Where is the desire for that golden sun of recognition?

Three Nashville ghostwriters shared their experiences, business models, writing know-how, and advice. And when they were asked that presumably hard question—*why*, each responded with an identical lack of hesitation: for the love of the work, of course.

Donna Peerce

Donna Peerce has been a ghostwriter and editor for fifteen years and during this time has ghostwritten, book doctored and/or edited over one hundred books. Several have been *New York Times* bestsellers and include both fiction and nonfiction. Two have been optioned for films and one is being produced as a TV series in the U.K. in 2016.

After beginning her career writing and producing for television shows and commercials, Peerce decided to branch into freelance editing and ghostwriting, crediting an ad she placed with *Writer's Digest* magazine for landing her first ghostwriting gig (which was "something about training puppies," Peerce remembers laughingly.) Now, Peerce manages fifteen to twenty projects at a time in nearly every genre, from memoirs, thought leadership, business, young adult fantasy and sci-fi, to graphic novels and film scripts. She has clients around the globe. Past international clients include those from France, Switzerland, Australia, Pakistan, Taiwan, India, China, the UK, and Germany—to name a few. When she's not traveling to work one-on-one with her clients, she writes for a full twelve hours a day, usually in her home office. "I work literally 24/7; this is my world....Sometimes, I have to remind myself to get up and eat," says Peerce. "But this is my absolute passion."

Rob Simbeck

In addition to ghostwriting seven books, Rob Simbeck is a writer, journalist, poet, songwriter, and editor. Simbeck got his start serving as editor for a Los Angeles magazine and writing for various newspapers. Simbeck's first ghostwriting gig was for an artist's fanclub newsletter in the 1980s: "I used to write his personal thoughts, without ever talking to him. I just made up his personal thoughts about what was going on."

His next ghostwriting opportunity came after he submitted a story of his own to *Guideposts* magazine, and although it was rejected, he got a surprising call: "They called me and said, 'Since you live in Nashville, if you can get a country star to work with you, we'll publish it. So I called Reba's office and we sat down for ninety minutes to find the thing that would be the hook for the story—which was when she first moved to Nashville and was really nervous, and her mother gave her a pep talk that convinced her to go to her first audition." Now, in addition to doing his own writing, Simbeck works with several Nashville publishing houses ghostwriting for clients who thus far have included pastors, the President of Dollar General, and the founder of Continental Insurance.

Kevin Kaiser

Kevin Kaiser started in investment business—a job that he says was essentially "managing money for rich families." But, says Kaiser, "I would get up in the morning and write books." And when he met a businessman name Ted Decker, who eventually asked him to move to Nashville to run his newly founded media company, Kaiser left his investment career. When the company later shut down, Kaiser decided to finally pursue his writing hobby as a career and began freelance writing comic books. Shortly, he was asked to be a brand manager for entertainment company Greater Trust where he used his business and marketing savvy to manage authors and got his first glimpses inside the editorial side of the business. Soon he began assisting writers with content development and story flow. In 2012, he left the company to be an independent ghostwriter and brand consultant and has since written six books that have appeared on the *New York Times* bestseller list and launched StorySellerU, a company that helps authors write and market their books.

How does this all work?

For Peerce, it is as simple as getting a call or email from a potential client with an idea for a book. She also works with several New York literary agents and Hollywood film producers who call her to ghostwrite books for people who have a great story but can't write. From the initial contact, Peerce says it is a matter of negotiating a fee and getting a contract signed. Peerce offers a tiered level of services depending on how much help the client wants and how much the client is willing to spend. The most basic level of service would be what Peerce calls *book doctor* services, a rewriting of a *mostly* fully-written rough draft; the next tier would be what most would call typical *ghostwriter* services, that is, developing and writing a book from either a client's basic idea or from a client's well-developed outline. Top tier service would see Peerce acting first as a ghostwriter and then, once the book is written, a *literary project manager*, where she is involved in getting the book published, including writing book proposals and/or pitching to literary agents and publishing houses. She has also written and produced video book trailers to promote books, much in the same way movie trailers promote films. Her fees range from twenty-five thousand to one hundred thousand dollars per book.

Most of her clients request a non-disclosure agreement, meaning Peerce is prohibited from disclosing the titles of many of the books she has written. "I cannot say one word. I can't tweet about the book, not one thing. For instance, one young adult fantasy sci-fi novel I ghosted was a huge success. I simply tweeted 'Hey, go buy this book; It's great.' Well, I got called by his attorneys saying, 'You are not allowed to say *one thing.*' Because the client, you know, didn't want anyone to know that someone had 'helped him' with the book—that someone had written it for him. So now, I am always careful. Very careful." But Peerce adds, for some books she *has* received credit, usually in the form of a line on the inside front page of the book reading, "Thank you so much to my writer and my friend, Donna Peerce."

Simbeck receives clients in two ways: through invitation from one of the publishing houses he works with, or from an independent client seeking a ghostwriter on his or her own. If the job is through a publishing house, Simbeck says there is a set fee, which he then has the choice to decline or accept. But if the client is independent, that is, finding him through word-of-mouth, or how I did—Google—Simbeck suggests his own fee up front and depending on the project may receive royalty payments as well. "Contracts are negotiable but usually I suggest one-third [of the payment] up front, one-third in six months, and one-third upon approval of the completed manuscript." He would not reveal his standard fee, but did add that his fees range from thirty thousand to one hundred thousand dollars, depending on the complexity of the book. Simbeck has actually never had a non-disclosure agreement and is sometimes even featured on the front cover of the final product with the qualifying statement, "as told to Rob Simbeck."

"There's no shame for them or me. It's a collaborative effort. They tell the story, and I craft it into a book," says Simbeck. Simbeck may be ghostwriting up to four books at once, and he has spent anywhere from six weeks to five years on a given project.

For Kaiser, the process begins when an author comes to him with an idea, often a very vague one. Kaiser and his client work together to flesh out the details of the story. "There's a lot of talking to get to know each other—there's a lot of that. And it's always a tug-of-war. 'I like that idea, I don't like that idea.'" But, Kaiser adds, "The author always wins. You have to remember it's their story, not yours." Kaiser's business and marketing background in the industry gives him a bit of an edge. While writing the story, he considers elements that are proven to make the book more marketable. "Every genre has "rules" that people expect. The key is: how can you bend those to make them more sellable?" says Kaiser. In the past, he has occasionally helped with getting a book he ghostwrote published. Although he would not reveal his standard payment, he says in his experience, compensation depends on the writer's level of experience, with a brand new ghostwriter earning about twenty thousand dollars per book and a practiced ghostwriter earning around two hundred thousand dollars per book.

How do you write like someone else?

Before Peerce begins a new project, she tries to get a sense of the client's natural voice—or better yet, what they *want* their voice to be. To do this, she spends a lot of time talking to her client and listening to the recordings of those interviews multiple times to determine their unique speaking patterns, vocabulary, and tone. Often, she travels to the client's location and meets with them regularly. "This helps tremendously," she says. She likes to ask them what author they believe they are most like and what type of books they read. In this way, a particular writing style begins to emerge. But developing a voice for the book is only the beginning; it's often up to Peerce to create the bulk of the content as well. "A lot of people think that ghostwriting is just fast-typing. They say, 'Oh, if you can type really fast, you can do this.' But it's so much more than that. Ghostwriting is eighty percent *thinking, dreaming, and research*. Twenty percent is the actual writing."

"I think you either have that empathy or you don't," answers Sim-

beck when asked how he manages to write in the voice of someone else.
Because many of his clients are non-writers, his process involves a lot
of listening to how they *speak* and learning their personal histories. In
this way, he is able to understand the elements that contributed to their
character and use that to develop an original voice. Simbeck exempli-
fies his process in a particular memoir he did for insurance giant, Randall Baskin. "Randall Baskin is a country guy, right? So the analogies are
going to be earthier than someone who went to seminary and is talking
about theology. There is a different vocabulary there."

Kaiser's clients are often writers themselves, so his work involves
less inventing and more mimicking the client's already well-developed
writing voice. He says he always starts by reading a lot of his client's
previous writing. But he has learned some tricks that help make the
process more methodical. For instance, he mentions a friend of his
who wanted to learn how to write like his favorite author—recreation-
ally, that is, not for a ghostwriting purpose. "I have a friend who wanted to write like Dean Koontz so he read all of Dean's books. Then he
chose his three favorite books....Then he just sat with the book next to
his computer and wrote the book—just *typed the book*, copied it, word-
for-word. And he could see the sequence of words, the patterns. He
said it was the most valuable lesson he ever learned in writing. He said,
'I thought I would just rush through it but no, I would stop and think,
'Ooh, why did he do it this way?' So that's one trick you can do."

Ghostwriting typically conjures that image of an invisible writer, but
it also affords a second, maybe more accurate interpretation: a writing
career that—like a ghost—can take illimitable forms, from bringing
to life a vague idea for a novel to transforming a pastor's sermon into
a book to memorializing a stranger's life. Peerce, Simbeck, and Kaiser
differ in many regards, but it seems that at least one sure conclusion
can be made: to be a successful ghostwriter, the only certain require-
ment is a passion for creating stories.

By Krista Walsh